I HEARD THE SNICK OF
A RIFLE LOCK...

...as if someone had cocked a hammer back. My blood froze and shivers sizzled up my spine like icy fingers stroking my back. I ducked and snaked my rifle from the cradle of the saddle and started to cock the lever.

"Do not move," a voice said, and I heard something scrape against a tree.

Dan and I both turned at the same time.

I saw movement, then a patch of color that looked like a deer. But it wasn't a deer. Because right above it, the black snout of a rifle seemed to grow right out of the tall pine tree. And the muzzle was pointed straight at me.

I knew then, that I was just a short trigger pull away from death.

Berkley titles by Jory Sherman

BLOOD RIVER

Jory Sherman

BERKLEY BOOKS, NEW YORK

THE BERKLEY PUBLISHING GROUP
Published by the Penguin Group
Penguin Group (USA) Inc.
375 Hudson Street, New York, New York 10014, USA
Penguin Group (Canada), 10 Alcorn Avenue, Toronto, Ontario M4V 3B2, Canada
(a division of Pearson Penguin Canada Inc.)
Penguin Books Ltd., 80 Strand, London WC2R 0RL, England
Penguin Group Ireland, 25 St. Stephen's Green, Dublin 2, Ireland (a division of Penguin Books Ltd.)
Penguin Group (Australia), 250 Camberwell Road, Camberwell, Victoria 3124, Australia
(a division of Pearson Australia Group Pty. Ltd.)
Penguin Books India Pvt. Ltd., 11 Community Centre, Panchsheel Park, New Delhi—110 017, India
Penguin Group (NZ), Cnr. Airborne and Rosedale Roads, Albany, Auckland 1310, New Zealand
(a division of Pearson New Zealand, Ltd.)
Penguin Books (South Africa) (Pty.) Ltd., 24 Sturdee Avenue, Rosebank, Johannesburg 2196, South Africa

Penguin Books Ltd., Registered Offices: 80 Strand, London WC2R 0RL, England

BLOOD RIVER

A Berkley Book / published by arrangement with the author

PRINTING HISTORY
Berkley edition / January 2005

ISBN: 0-425-19991-6

BERKLEY®
Berkley Books are published by The Berkley Publishing Group,
a division of Penguin Group (USA) Inc.,
375 Hudson Street, New York, New York 10014.
BERKLEY is a registered trademark of Penguin Group (USA) Inc.
The "B" design is a trademark belonging to Penguin Group (USA) Inc.

PRINTED IN THE UNITED STATES OF AMERICA

10 9 8 7 6 5 4 3 2 1

For Norma Wilkinson,
the Belle of Oaklea Mansion
in Winnsboro, Texas

Keep your fears to yourself,
But share your courage with others.

—ROBERT LOUIS STEVENSON

1

THE COMANCHES FILLED OUR HEARTS WITH TERROR IN THOSE days. They drove us from our home in Texas, not all of a sudden, but gradually, as our fear gripped us like an iron hand squeezing our throats, over a period of time. They were like our own shadows, attached to us, and it seemed we could never escape them. They were our shadows and they clung to us no matter how fast we ran.

In the beginning they were a nuisance along that particular stretch of the Palo Duro Canyon, south of Amarillo. They stole from our gardens, they snatched our chickens off their roosts, butchered our pigs and goats. They rustled our cattle and ran off our horses. Pa said it was part of the price we had to pay for being allowed to live in a beautiful country where grass grew and waters flowed and the sky was so big and blue it made you feel blessed to live under its immense canopy.

We did not know, at first, how bad it was going to get with the Comanches. I think Pa thought he could buy them off with cattle and trinkets. Ma thought they would just go away, or that the Texas Rangers would someday come to that part of Texas and kill them all.

My mother taught me most of what I know. She was a smart woman and she wanted me to be smart. She taught me books and writing and poetry and my numbers and a whole lot more. I didn't have any formal schooling because we lived in a wild part of Texas and town was so far away we seldom went there. I guess we would have stayed in Texas forever if it hadn't been for the Comanches who tried their best to kill us and all but stole us blind before my pa had the sense to take us away from there.

"I don't want our scalps to hang in some red savage's lodge," Pa told us.

But, the truth was, he was scared of the Comanches and so was I. Not my mother, though. She wanted to stay and fight for our land after the war, saying that we had paid dearly for it and we should not allow the Comanches to run us off. There was a big argument about leaving and I heard it all one night just before we left. I think that's when I began to think about bravery and courage because I surely thought my father was a coward, afraid of his own shadow.

"Keith," my mother said, "you just can't pick up and drive two hundred head of cattle up north and leave this place to the savages."

"Mercy," my father said, "I talked to our neighbor, Leon Carrero, last week who said there's plenty of good grazing land up in Jefferson Territory and I aim to go there. We can start over."

"What was Leon doing over here?" Ma asked.

"He's losing his place, too. Mano Rojo's Comanches. He said he's thinkin' about goin' up north to the mountains. He's mighty scared. He says the Comanches are gettin' bolder by the day. A bunch of 'em rode up the other day and filled their skin bags with water from his well and then they took all his eggs and demanded that he give them tobacco. That's mighty bold, if you ask me."

"Well, you can go without me and Chip. We're staying."

My father, unlike my mother, didn't have much schooling, but I always thought of him as a practical man. Except I didn't like the idea of leaving Texas either and I thought he was being a fool to even mention it. But I had been taught respect, by my ma, of course, and so I didn't say anything that night. I just listened to the folks argue.

"You know I can't do that, Mercy. I love you and Chip and I want you to come with me. Before we all get killed."

"The Texas Rangers have all but killed off most of the Apaches and a whole lot of the Comanches in south and east Texas, up near the Red. They won't bother us much longer, Keith. Just have patience."

"Well, if the Rangers are running the Apaches and the Comanches off, old Mano Rojo sure as hell hasn't heard about it. Him and his bunch drove off ten more head of beef yesterday. I'm tired of feeding his renegades."

"Well, maybe if you shot him, he wouldn't be so quick to steal from us," she said.

"Hell, the Comanches outnumber us. I ain't goin' to do a fool thing like that."

"Well, maybe I'll shoot him with my rifle," my ma said. She was a petite woman, but she was wiry and strong. She was beautiful, too, with her flaxen hair and sky blue eyes.

My heart soared when I heard her say that. I was turning twenty-two and she had taught me to shoot a rifle when I was eight years old and a pistol when I was ten. She was a crack shot, but then, so was my father. I think she taught him to shoot firearms, too.

"Mercy, you do not see the danger. The Comanches will kill us all if we don't leave. Leon knows them better than we do. He says they are no longer just stealing. They want to kill the whites."

"I know they are dangerous, Keith. But we have Luke and Barney. They will fight alongside us."

"What we pay them, I couldn't ask them to risk their lives for us."

"We give them food and shelter and pay them what we can."

Luke Neeley and Barney Wiggs worked for my father. They were both widowers and Pa found them in Amarillo, willing to work. They knew cattle and both were good men. I didn't know how they were as fighters, however. Luke was a wise man, though, and said he had fought with Colonel Rip Ford in the war as a cavalryman. Barney didn't seem to have much sense, but he was a good enough worker.

"Mercy, if something happens, don't say I didn't warn you. We'll stay. For now. But, at the first sign of trouble, I'm takin' you north."

"Let's just leave it at that, then," my mother said sweetly and Pa stopped his arguing. He moped around for a few days, but things were quiet and he did not bring up the subject again. We were working pretty hard at spring roundup and didn't even think about the Comanches until one day when a rancher's boy came running up to the house just at dusk, scared plumb out of his wits.

"Why who could that be?" Ma asked, when she saw the boy running toward us as if his pants were on fire.

"That's Jamie Long," I said. "Virgil Long's boy. Why he lives a good five mile from here, Ma."

Pa was washing up at the pump out front, but he saw Jamie, too, and he stood there gaping at the boy, who was no more than twelve, as if he was seeing a ghost.

"Come quick," Jamie gasped, as he ran up to the porch. "Ma and Pa need you. Comanches."

Then, Jamie fell to the ground, gasping for breath. His face was white as a linen coverlet and his lips were bluish. I think he was a sickly child.

"Chip," Pa said, "go fetch Luke and Barney and tell them to saddle our horses. Mercy, get our rifles and pistols. Quick."

Luke and Barney were all worn out, but when I told them what had happened, they were wide awake. The three of us saddled all the horses real quick and by the time we got to the house, Pa and Ma were ready. She gave me my rifle and I strapped on my pistol.

"Jamie can ride with you, Chip," Pa said.

By then, Jamie was able to breathe and he climbed up behind me in the saddle. We rode that five miles to his folks' place in good time, pacing all the horses so that none got winded or sweated so much as to founder.

It was near dark when we rode up to the Long place. My stomach knotted up right away when Pa reined up in front of the small frame house with its little white picket fence. It was just too quiet and still, as if the dusk had hushed everything when all the long shadows and the puddles of shadows became just one dark patch. It was like walking into a graveyard. Nothing moved. Nobody called out. Behind me, I could feel Jamie shivering.

"Where's your pa and ma, Jamie?" I asked him, my voice low and husky with either dust or some emotion I couldn't explain right well just then.

"I dunno," he said. "They was runnin' from the Comanches. Over toward the barn."

The barn stood as silent as the rest of the place. I heard the rattle of rifle levers as Pa, Luke, and Barney dismounted, jerking their weapons free of their scabbards. The sounds were enough to send chills up my spine. I drew my rifle from its sheath, helped Jamie climb down and then I slid out of the saddle.

"Pa," I said, "Jamie said he saw his folks running toward the barn to escape the Comanches."

"It's mighty quiet," Pa said. "Mercy, you better keep the

boy here whilst me and the boys walk over to that barn and take a gander."

"Jamie, come here," Ma said, lighting down from her bay mare. "We'll let the men look for your folks."

Jamie ran to her and I fell into step behind my pa, Luke, and Barney. I caught up with Luke and stayed a step behind.

"What do you think, Luke?" I asked.

"It don't look good, Chip. You keep your eyes peeled."

"You think the Comanches are in the barn?"

"I don't reckon. It don't sound like anything's alive in that barn. Not even the horses Long keeps."

Luke was right. Long's horses would have whinnied or neighed or something. There wasn't a sound and the barn doors were wide open like some giant gaping maw. Pa got there first and he stayed to one side of those open doors and called in as he waved us all to get out of the way.

"Anybody in there? Virgil? Ho there, Virgil."

There was no answer.

"Shit," Barney said.

"Can't see a damned thing in there," Pa said.

"I'll go in," Luke said. "Cover me."

Without waiting for an answer, Luke hunched over and levered a round from his Winchester '73 into the chamber. He ran inside real quick and we all waited, hardly breathing at all so we could listen real careful. I could hear Luke's boots crunching the loose straw and then he must have stopped because I didn't hear him anymore.

A minute or two later, we all heard something and then we saw a golden light shining inside the barn.

"Keith, you better come in here," Luke said.

Barney, Pa, and I went inside the barn, treading as if we were walking on eggs. Luke had lit a lantern and was standing there next to something on the ground, holding the lantern high up so that he could see. The lamp cast shadows and the shadows moved like wraiths. It was very spooky in all that quiet and what was lying on the ground wasn't a horse or any animal, but a man.

"It's Virgil Long," Luke said, "and he ain't pretty."

Virgil had been scalped. There was a circular cut at the front of his skull and a large chunk of hair missing from a bloody bald patch.

"They cut his nuts off," Barney said, and I looked down at Virgil's crotch. His pants were cut open and where his genitals had been there was only a gouge filled with blood. I was sick looking at it and had to turn away and take a deep breath to keep from losing everything I had in my stomach.

"That ain't the worst," Luke said.

Pa just stood there, staring at Virgil's corpse, his eyes cloudy and distant, his face washed of all color. The copper light from the lamp illuminated his ghastly visage.

Luke kicked a partially opened stall door and it widened. Inside, on filthy straw, lay the nude body of a woman. She had been butchered. Her body was contorted because it was obvious that they had broken both her legs and bent them at odd angles. Her private parts had been cut away and all the hair on her head had been torn off so that nothing remained except a thin film of bone-white flesh stippled with blood. Her nose had been cut off and her mouth smashed. Worse, she had been gutted, so that her belly was wide open and another place where her heart had been was just an empty hole. There was blood everywhere.

"We know who did this, too," Luke said, pointing to the rear of the stall.

There, on the back wall, was a bloody handprint.

"That's old Mano Rojo's signature," Luke said. "Red Hand. Plain as day. Christ."

My stomach was roiling and I tasted bile in my throat. There was a noise behind me and when I turned around, there was Ma standing there, gazing down at Mrs. Long's desecrated and mutilated body. She gasped in horror and brought a hand to her mouth.

"Laverne," she gasped. "It's Laverne Long, isn't it?"

"Yes'm," Luke said.

Pa turned to Ma and, instead of offering her comfort, just glared at her.

"Now, maybe you'll listen to reason," Pa said. "That could have been me out there and you down here."

"You bastard," Ma spat and slapped Pa across the face.

Then she turned and ran out of the barn, leaving us all standing there in a deep silence.

"Keith, you and the missus go on back," Luke said. "Barney and I will clean all this up. I'm thinking Red Hand won't be back tonight."

"No, but where will he strike next?" Pa said.

Nobody answered.

"You go on back, too, Chip," Luke said to me. "Take that Long boy with you. He's going to need some comfortin'." Then, he added, "Along with your ma, I reckon."

Pa stalked out of the stall and left the barn. I took one last look at Virgil Long and fought down the sickness that threatened to rise up in my throat. I had never seen anything like this. Had never seen death up so close or so horrible. I tried to imagine what kind of a man would do these things to another human being.

As I left that place, I had no answers.

2

THAT WAS NOT TO BE THE LAST WE HEARD OF RED HAND, the Comanche chief. In fact, he paid us a visit while Ma and Pa were taking Jamie Long up to his aunt Michelle's in Amarillo. Luke, Barney, and me were routing out strays and calves from the deep brush in the Palo Duro one blazing hot afternoon, when we heard a commotion up on the plain.

Luke rode up to the rim while Barney and I were putting the Flying M brand on two calves we had caught. The calves were bawling and their mothers raising a ruckus so we didn't hear much down there. Luke came riding back down to tell us to come and take a look. We let the calves go back to their mothers on spindly legs that put wobbles in their hind ends and caught up our horses. We rode up to the top of the rim and looked in the direction Luke was pointing.

There was a huge dust cloud rising up, all reddish and pale brown.

"Ain't that where we had a herd a-grazin'?" Barney asked.

"That herd is being driven," Luke said. "If you look real close up ahead of the dust, you'll see some naked red bodies on ponies goin' in and out. They must be runnin' off fifty head."

"Let's go catch 'em," I said.

"That's Red Hand's bunch, Chip," Luke said. "Now look behind the dust cloud and you'll see he's got braves back there waitin' for us to do just that."

Sure enough, there were at least a dozen Comanches with rifles riding around behind the cloud of dust, pumping their weapons up and down as if daring us to come after them. I counted ten or twelve and then a whole bunch more up in front of the dust and a line of cattle streaming off into the distance. In a few moments, the cows and Comanches were all gone, disappeared over the horizon; the dust hung in the air like an ominous red cloud as if to mark their passing.

I watched numbly as all our hard work drifted away, disappeared over the horizon. My family was counting on the money those cattle would raise to feed and clothe us, and now, the Comanches had taken that money out of our pockets as surely as if they had robbed us at gunpoint.

"We have to go after them, Luke," I said. "We have to get those cattle back."

"I'm thinkin' Red Hand might just want us to chase after him," Luke said.

"Then let's do it."

"Chip, you might want to study on that notion before you go off half-cocked."

"Pa will blame us for this, and he'll be real bad hurt to lose that many head at once."

"I'm wondering why the Comanches have done got so bold. And, that's a heap of cattle to run off at one time."

Luke was staring into the distance, looking at that cloud of dust that just hung there in the sky as if a dozen cannons had gone off and killed everything around that place. Slowly, the cloud began to come apart as the fine red dust sifted back down to earth, leaving even more of an emptiness.

"I wonder where Red Hand is taking them," I said. "He doesn't have a ranch to go to. Would he sell them, you think?"

"I expect he's taking them up into the territories. Maybe to sell them. Maybe to a tribe."

"A tribe?"

"The Comanches are scattered all over. Some up in Indian Territory, maybe some up in Kansas. I don't know. He might be feeding a lot of his kin someplace. In a ways, it don't make no sense, him rustling that many cattle."

"I say we go after him and get those cows back. Damn, Luke. We have to do something."

"Chip, did you see what was in Virgil's mouth when he was laid out in his barn?"

"No, I just looked at the top of his head where his hair used to be."

"Red Hand and his bunch stuffed dirt in poor old Virgil's mouth."

"Dirt? Why?"

Barney came up then, and he didn't look too well.

"The Comanches want us out of here," Barney said. "Puttin' dirt in a dead man's mouth means they considered the Long family trespassers on their land. I'm gettin' the hell out, 'fore I end up with a mouth full of dirt myself."

"What do you mean?" I asked.

"I'm lightin' a shuck for other parts, Chip. Red Hand done give us a message. And, I'm done readin' it."

"Barney, you can't leave now. It just wouldn't be right. At least wait until Pa and Ma get back from Amarillo."

"Nope. That might be too late. Luke, you understand, don't you? Why I got to leave now?"

"Sure, Barney. You're a damned coward."

Luke spoke real pleasant-like, but his meaning was plain. Barney's face blanched as if he had been slapped. His lower lip quivered and for a minute, I thought he was going to ball up a fist and lay into Luke, but he just stood there, his hands trembling.

"Damn you, Luke," he said. "I ain't no damned coward. But I ain't no fool, neither. Them damned Comanches mean to drive us all out or kill us, and I got better things to do than wind up dead."

"You can't draw your pay, Barney," Luke said. "Not until Keith gets back."

"Can you loan me some money and take it out of what I got comin'?"

"Nope," Luke said. He pulled his pockets inside out to show Barney that he was broke.

"Well, you tell Keith Morgan he can send my pay to me in care of General Delivery down to San Antonio. I'm goin' down thataway."

"Suit yourself," Luke said.

"I hope you get scalped on the way down there, Barney," I said.

"Sonny," Barney said, "you got some lip on you, but I don't give a damn. You'll be squalling loud enough when them Comanches come back for your scalp."

I started to go for Barney then, but Luke grabbed me and held me back. Barney went back down in the brush and caught up his horse. In a few minutes he was riding back toward the ranch to get his bedroll, clothes, and possibles out of the bunkhouse.

"Good riddance," I said, my temper still flaring like a flame at a bonfire. "The damned coward."

Luke put a hand on my shoulder.

"Chip, you don't want to be calling Barney a coward like that."

"Well, you did."

"That's different. I know he's a coward, firsthand. But I didn't call him that to shame him. I was hoping that he'd stick it out here and not run away again. Besides, Barney asked me about courage more than once."

"Why?"

"He said he didn't have none. And he was scared of dying. He was court-martialed during the war for running away from a battle when he was with the 2nd Texas over in Corinth."

"I don't know what courage is myself, Luke."

"Me neither. Barney asked me how I got over my fear in battle."

"And, what did you tell him?"

"I said I never got over being afraid. I wanted to run, too. More than once."

"Why didn't you?"

"I think you start thinking of letting somebody else down. If I run off when the fighting's real bad, I might get the man next to me killed."

"So, what did you tell Barney about courage and fear?" I asked.

"I told him fear came from thinking just about himself and that courage came from thinking about other folks."

"That might be hard to do if somebody is shooting at you. If somebody is trying to kill you."

"It's not something you think about, really. If somebody's trying to kill you, you got to think about killing them first. Maybe that's how you get courage, Chip. You just do what has to be done and that drives away the fear."

"Maybe Barney is just being practical. He doesn't want to die and so he gets away from what might kill him."

"That may be why Barney is a coward. He runs off every time he's in danger. So, he's never had to fight fear, you know. Unless a man faces up to what scares him, he's always going to be scared."

I thought about what Luke said that day many times and wondered if I'd ever have courage. When I thought about what Red Hand did to Virgil, I felt real fear, way down deep inside me. I didn't want to die like that. And, I thought about what Virgil and his wife's last moments of life might have been like, when they knew they were going to die horribly and get cut up and be scalped. They had to be mighty scared and I wouldn't fault a person for being afraid at such times.

I was afraid to go after Red Hand and try and get those cattle back. But, Luke told me that if we had done that, it wouldn't be courageous—just reckless and foolish. I was happy to agree with him. I knew that if he and I tried to fight so many Comanches, we wouldn't have a chance. We would have been killed.

But, I wondered after that if I wasn't a coward myself, just like Barney.

3

PA WAS MIGHTY MAD WHEN HE AND MA GOT BACK FROM Amarillo and found out those cattle had been rustled by Comanches. He told me and Luke to make a tally and find out just how many head Red Hand had stolen. Near as we could figure, the Comanches made off with fifty-two head, which reduced our herd by a quarter.

For a day or two, Pa kicked buckets and slammed down pitchforks in the barn and grumped around the house like a wounded bear until Ma told him if he slammed one more door or kicked one more chair, she was going to nail him to a tree and set the tree on fire. He helped me and Luke finish roundup, but he took no satisfaction in a job well done. He was still mad at Barney, too, and said he wasn't going to send his pay to him, which I thought was just plain mean and told Ma about it.

She finally sent off the money owed Barney with the Carreros on their next trip up to Amarillo. Leon was still talking about moving up to Jefferson Territory and Pa brought it up nearly every night at supper, which caused more arguments and made me want to sleep out in the bunkhouse with Luke. But I just went to my bunk in the house and read books and practiced writing on the tablets Ma had bought me. I think I used too many flowery words, but I loved words and when I found one I didn't know I looked it up in the Webster's dictionary and started keeping lists of all the new words I was learning. I tried learning at least three new words a day, which was pretty fascinating to me.

Things were pretty quiet for a while, and I was beginning to think we'd seen the last of Red Hand and the Comanches. If so, fifty head of cattle was still a small price to pay to get rid of him. Leon said he'd heard that Red Hand had been driven across the Red up into Kansas, but that was only a rumor going around Amarillo, Pa thought. Luke said that Red Hand might have gone up into Kansas all right, but more likely he had driven our cattle up there and sold them cheap. When I asked him if he thought the Comanches would bother us any more, he just shrugged and wouldn't answer.

One day, though, we had a visitor and he put us all on edge.

Ma spotted several riders on the skyline, some distance from the house and called out to Pa and me.

"Riders coming."

Pa and I looked up, saw several riders on the road. Then, one of them broke off and rode down the lane to our house, while the others rode on toward Carrero's spread and maybe to other ranchers beyond Leon's ranch.

"What the hell . . ." Pa said.

Ma left the porch and went on inside the house. I knew she'd be standing near a window with a rifle or scattergun in her hand until she found out who the stranger was and what he wanted. It was something she had learned to do a long time ago. Not that she was overly suspicious of strangers, it was just a precaution some folks used on the remote ranches. I don't know what she would have done if all of the riders had turned down our lane, but I was keeping my eyes on the other riders until they dropped over the horizon and disappeared.

The horsemen were all carrying bedrolls tied to the backs of their cantles. Something flashed on their chests, reflecting the sun. They were not out for a Sunday ride.

The man approaching was also wearing something shiny on the front of his shirt. Like the other riders, two rifles jutted out of scabbards on either side of his saddle, and his saddlehorn dripped with gunbelts carrying sidearms in holsters.

"What do you think, Pa?" I asked.

"Those look like rangers to me."

"Mr. Morgan," the man said, as he rode up. "I'm Fargo, with the Texas Rangers."

"Light down, Mr. Fargo."

"I won't be that long. I just rode by to inform you that you folks may be in danger here. From Comanches."

"Hell, we been in danger from Comanches ever since we set down stakes here."

"You might want to take this warning a little more seriously, Mr. Morgan. Red Hand, a Comanche chief, is on the warpath. We think he may be heading this way."

"Hell, he stole more'n fifty head of my cattle nigh a month ago. Why didn't you boys catch him?"

"We know about Red Hand's depredations, sir. He drove those cattle, and other stolen head, up into Kansas, and sold them. He bought guns and ammunition with the proceeds and he's gathered him a bunch of renegade Apaches and Kiowas into a small army of savages. And he's heading this way, we believe."

"You believe? Hell, don't you know?"

"Sir, Red Hand believes this land belongs to his people.

We know that. So, naturally, we expect him to come back down here. This time, in force."

"Mr. Fargo," I said. "He had more than a dozen, maybe two dozen braves with him when he rustled our stock."

"Well, he's got fifty or sixty warriors ready to paint up, son."

Ma stepped out of the house and crossed the porch, descended the steps. She walked over to the ranger and looked up at him.

"Are you here to defend us, Mr. Fargo, or just warn us?"

"We're hoping to get a troop up to Amarillo to go after Red Hand, ma'am. In the meantime, I'm just warning you."

"What's your first name, Mr. Fargo?" Ma asked.

"Why, Fordham, ma'am. Folks call me Ford."

"Well, Ford, we thank you kindly for the warning. But we've stood our ground against Red Hand and we're not afraid of him."

"Yes'm." Fargo touched the brim of his hat in a kind of salute to her. "I just think you and your family ought to clear out for a time. Until we can get enough rangers down this way to drive the Comanches out of Texas once and for all."

Ma snorted in disbelief.

"Well, Ford Fargo, you've done your duty. Now, we have work to do. I wish you good luck in warning all the other ranchers hereabouts. I'm sure they'll be as relieved as we are to know that you are mindful of our safety."

"Yes'm," Fargo said. "I just wish you'd take my advice and ride up to Amarillo until this is over. You'll be safe there."

"We're safe here, Ford Fargo," Ma said. "And no ranger has ever come by here before you. Which makes me wonder what it takes to get protection for our land and cattle."

"We're spread pretty thin, Mrs. Morgan."

"Then I suggest you summon more rangers to help you kill or capture those Comanches."

"We're trying, ma'am."

Ma gave out a scornful laugh. Fargo's face wrinkled with a look of distaste, as if he had tasted something vile.

"I hope you succeed, Mr. Fargo," she said.

Ma turned away from him as if to walk back toward the house. Then something caught her eye. She looked to the north. Fargo turned his horse and he saw it too. Pa and I looked where Ma was looking. My blood seemed to freeze in my veins and my heart began to pound, throbbing like a drum at my temples.

"Smoke," Pa said.

"That's Virgil's place," Ma said. She shot an accusing look at the ranger.

"What did you do, burn down the Long place?" she asked.

"Of course not," Fargo said. "We passed by there. It was deserted."

"Well, it's not deserted now, is it, Mr. Fargo?"

"Damn," Fargo said. Then he touched the brim of his hat in a farewell salute. "That's what he's doing, ma'am, burning down the houses he's attacked. We found another one further up toward Amarillo. I've got to go."

"Wait," Ma said. "Which house was burned?"

"The Salsbury place. Folks there were run out two weeks ago, two of the hands killed and scalped."

Ma looked at Pa. He shook his head in disbelief.

"We saw them when we took Jamie Long up to Amarillo," Ma said. "They seemed fine and happy."

Fargo didn't hear. He was already slapping leather, racing his horse down the lane back to the road. He left a column of dust in his wake. At the road, he turned right and I knew he was going after the other rangers. But he would be too late to do anything.

I knew Ed Salsbury and his wife, Frieda. I was glad they were alive. As for their hands, I hadn't known them, but I remembered that they were young, probably not even in their twenties. It was hard to think of them being dead, harder even to think of them being scalped. And now there was no trace of the Salsburys up north. It was as if they had never lived there. And now the Long place was burning. I looked at our house and shuddered inside. We had built it with our own hands and it wasn't right that a Comanche could just burn it down. I hoped Ma would heed the ranger's warning and listen to Pa. But I knew she wouldn't. When her back was up, she would stand and fight. Not run away.

"That's what will happen to our house, if we leave," Ma said. "The damned Comanches will burn it to the ground."

"Mercy, at least the Salsburys are alive. The Longs would be too if they had left sooner. We're next."

"Keith, if you let fear rule your life, you'll always be prey to merciless savages and scoundrels, be they white or red. As long as we're here and can fight, the Comanches will never burn down our house and take our land."

"We can't fight off fifty Comanches, Mercy."

"There are four of us here, and the house is built solid. We can defend it, Keith. We just have to think smarter than Red Hand, and shoot a lot straighter than his braves."

"Four against fifty?" Pa said.

Ma said nothing. She turned back toward the column of smoke rising in the sky. I wondered what she was thinking at that moment. Was she seeing our own house going up in flames? Or was she wondering how long it would take the Comanches to ride five miles and start attacking us?

She turned to me.

"Chip, you'd better go get Luke and tell him to move into the house with us. Have him bring his rifles and pistols and be ready to stay a spell."

Pa lifted his hands in exasperation.

"Mercy . . ." he began.

She whirled on him, her eyes flashing.

"Keith, you'd better start filling buckets with water from the well and bring them into the house. I will not be burned out of my own home by a bunch of mindless red savages."

Then Ma stalked off and went inside the house.

I sniffed the air. I could smell the smoke now as some of it drifted toward us. It smelled of death and destruction and made my stomach turn. What would happen to us now? Were we all going to die like the Longs? I scanned the horizon, expecting to see painted Comanches riding toward us at full speed, screaming their war songs, yipping like coyotes running after deer.

But I saw nothing but empty land and sky, and a pall of smoke that hung over the Long place and was creeping our way. I thought that now we were at that place mentioned in the Bible, the valley of the shadow of death.

4

LUKE NEELEY MOVED INTO THE MAIN HOUSE WITH US, BUNKED in my room. He was a man who valued his privacy, so he didn't like it much, but I was glad to have him there. I liked talking to him and he was generous with his wisdom.

"I notice you been practicin' a lot with that Colt .44, Chip. That's a pretty big pistol for a skinny feller like you."

Startled, I looked at Luke, who was sitting on the edge of the bunk bed, rolling a quirly.

"It feels good in my hand."

"Not too good, I hope. I'd hate to see you take a wrong turn in the trail."

"What do you mean, Luke?"

"A gun can shape a man's life."

"I just want to be a good pistol shot."

"And you are. I've noticed."

"So what are you driving at, Luke?"

He folded the paper around the tobacco so that he had a tight roll. Then he licked the edge of the paper at the fold, giving it a tight seal. He stuck the end of the cigarette between his lips and began looking for a match, patting his shirt pockets.

"A lucifer?" he said.

"I keep the matches in that box under my bed."

"Let's go outside." Luke bent down, found the matches. He struck one on my bedpost and lit his quirly. Then we walked outside into the embers of the sunset. The bullbats were flying, their silver dollars flashing on their wings. I had my own door to my room and it led out in back of the house. The reason I had two beds in there was because I had had a baby brother who died of pneumonia when he was two years old. Pa had built a bed for him when I was only six or seven. James Digger had never slept in it.

"A man who takes up the gun," Luke continued, "will always have a shadow following him. You kill a man in public, it becomes a public matter. People talk. The story gets bigger and bigger and you get a reputation. The reputation flows everywhere like a big stain on a flat floor and pretty soon some young gunny comes out of that shadow and tries to steal your reputation at gunpoint."

"I don't plan on being a gunman," I said.

"Good. A gun is a tool, just like a hammer or a hatchet. But it can also give a man a sense of power if it's used wrong."

"A sense of power?"

"The power of life and death."

"I see."

"Do you, Chip? Power can be a bad thing, you know. A man starts thinking he's above the law or beyond the law, he's headed for big trouble."

"I don't want that kind of power, Luke. Don't worry."

"I ain't worried. Now, this Comanche business, that's something else. It's not going to go away, you know."

"I know. Pa's pretty worried. He wants to move off our land and go up north."

"He's spoke to me about it. Jefferson Territory. The Rocky Mountains. The dream."

"Huh?"

"Keith's got him a dream and it keeps getting bigger every day. Your ma is worried too, you know. Oh, she don't show it none, but she is. But she's a nester."

"A nester?"

"Like a bird. She's made herself a nest here and she don't want to give it up. She'll fight like a she-cat to protect her little nest."

"I know she will. I wish those Comanches would just go away."

"Thing is," Luke said, "there's Injuns up in the mountains, too, and in between here and there. You can't run away from all of them. What most people hereabouts forget is that we're sitting on their land. They were here first."

"But they're bad. They do horrible things to people. Like the Longs. Scalping and murdering."

"Same as white folk done to them when they first came out here to Texas. And everywhere else. The Comanches are fighting for their land. Land we took away from them."

"They could have their own land if they wanted. They're just lazy and no damned good."

"You think so, Chip? Naw, they ain't lazy. They just lived different, that's all. They had all the land to themselves and was free to go where they wanted. Then we come along and tell them they can't come on to our property. We mark it off and fence it off and it's like we chopped their legs off."

"I don't see it that way, Luke."

"No, and the Comanches don't see it your way, neither."

"The Comanches don't obey our laws. That's the whole trouble."

"Would you obey their laws?"

I thought about that for a minute or two. I tried to think

how it would be if the shoe was on the other foot. What if we wanted their cattle and their horses and their land? What if they said we had to obey their laws or they would kill us?

"It would be hard."

"It's hard for them, too. If you and your family go up to Jefferson Territory, you'll run into other kinds of injuns just as fierce as the Comanches, just as mean and hard-headed. That's all I'm tryin' to say. You go someplace else, you generally take your troubles with you."

"But we want to live in peace," I said.

"So do the Comanches. But their way, not ours."

"If we do move up there, Luke, will you come with us?"

"I don't know," he said. "I'd have to study on it a while."

If we did drive cattle up to the mountains, I sure wanted Luke along. I didn't know how me, Ma, and Pa could drive a hundred and fifty head way up there into Jefferson Territory.

Pa didn't like Luke being in the house at all. He said it made him nervous to have another man in the house and put a cramp in his nightly affectionate behavior toward Ma. At mealtimes, though, we were like one big happy family.

A week went by, with no sign of the Comanches. Then, one morning, we saw riders approaching from the east. My heart raced because I recognized them right away, almost as soon as they appeared on the horizon.

"Who's that?" Pa asked.

"It's Leon Carrero," I said.

"Who's that with him?"

"Why, I think that's his daughter, Nora, Pa." I knew damned well it was Nora and I felt guilty because I hadn't been over to see her since the Longs had died. She was a beautiful woman, two years younger than I, and I had been sweet on her ever since she stopped wearing pigtails.

Leon's father was Spanish, from Cadiz, and his mother Irish, born in County Cork, Ireland. So Nora had dusky skin and bright blue eyes like Ma's, and hair the color of a fading sunset, russet in winter, more golden in summer when the sun bleached out the red. I planned to marry Nora one day, but I hadn't told anyone about that, not even Nora.

My heart was pounding by the time Leon and Nora rode up. Ma came out of the house, and met us all at the pump where Pa and I were washing up for lunch. Luke was off riding fence in one of the pastures.

"Leon, you and Nora are just in time for lunch," Ma said. "Nora, you pretty thing, light down and let me take a look at you."

Leon and Nora dismounted. I took the reins from their horses and tied them to a hitch post off to the side of the yard. Nora gave my mother a hug. Pa and Leon shook hands.

"We can't stay too long," Leon said. "I just came by to tell you me and Kathleen and Nora are driving our herd up to Kansas. Then we're going on over to Jefferson Territory with that part of the herd we don't sell in Kansas."

"You're right smart, Leon," Pa said. "Wish I was goin' with you."

"You ought to, Keith. Them Texas Rangers plumb scared the hell out of me. You hear what happened to the Salsburys?"

Pa nodded as I walked back over and stood there, staring at Nora.

The sun struck her hair just right, spun copper and gold threads through it like shining wires, and made her face shimmer. Her blue eyes met mine and I felt a tug at my loins, something that always happened when I was around her. She was so pretty, she made my insides melt.

"We heard," Pa said.

"Well, we're packin' up," Leon said. "I'm going to drive eighty or ninety head up to Abilene in Kansas, along with what horses I got left, sell some there and drive the rest to Jefferson Territory."

"When?" Pa asked.

"In a week or so."

"How does Kathleen feel about this?" Ma asked.

Leon shuffled his feet, looked down at the ground. "She don't like it none too much, leavin' her home and all, but she don't want no harm to come to us, neither."

"You're asking a lot of her, Leon," Ma said.

"Not when you think about what happened to the Longs and now the Salsburys have pulled out. The writing is on the wall, Mercy."

"If it is, then you scribbled it on there," Ma said.

"Mercy," Pa said, "ain't no call to be rude to Leon. Leon, I think you're doin' the right thing."

Behind Leon, Nora was shaking her head, ever so slightly. So, I knew she didn't want to go. I didn't want her to go, either.

"I know I am," Leon said. "Kathleen wanted to come over here with us, but she's busy packin' and said for me to say her good-byes. She said she gets too emotional and all. You know."

"I understand," Ma said. "You tell her I wish her well. You, too, Leon."

"Yes'm. She said you'd understand."

"What about Indians up there?" I asked. "Not only in the mountains, but all across the prairie?"

Pa shot me a dirty look. Ma looked surprised. So did Nora.

"They got forts all over Kansas, I hear. And we're not going far enough north to run into the Sioux and Cheyenne. The Rangers said the Army was going to kill all the Indians out west. They said the Army was sending a general to wipe out the Sioux, someone named Custer. I expect we'll be safe enough where we're going."

Pa turned to Ma.

"We ought to be going with them, Mercy. There's safety in numbers. What do you think, Leon?"

"Kathleen was hoping I could talk you folks into coming with us. It would make it a mite safer, for sure. And we'd surely welcome the company. I know Kathleen would."

"So would I," Nora said, and there was a husk in her voice as if she was close to tears.

"I think we ought to go with them, too," I said. "Ma, we can't just wait around here for the Comanches to come and slaughter us."

"I will not be driven from my land," Ma said. "We'll make do where we are."

"She's mighty stubborn," Pa said, and I realized how lame he was up against her. Sometimes I wished he showed more backbone than he did.

"So you won't change your mind, Mercy," Leon said.

Ma shook her head.

Nora's eyes welled up and I walked over to her, took her hand. I put my arm around her waist and squeezed her. She turned and fell into my arms, sobbing. Leon looked ill at ease. Pa scowled and Ma came over and patted Nora on the back.

"Look what you're doing to your family, Leon," Ma said. "You just don't know how hard it is to leave your home."

"I know, Mercy. I hate it worse than anything I've ever done. I just don't want to see my girls murdered and scalped by Red Hand. I 'spect we'll all cry some before we pick up the last stake."

Ma turned and started toward the house. "I wish you well, Leon. You tell Kathleen . . . well, tell her I wish she wasn't going away. Good-bye and good luck to all of you."

Ma was starting to cry, too. I held Nora close and she whispered into my ear.

"Chip, please come with us. I love you."

"I love you, too, Nora," I whispered and then she kissed me on the cheek and dried the tears from her eyes.

"Pa, let's go back," Nora said.

Pa and Leon shook hands. We watched Leon and Nora climb back onto their horses and ride away. We waved at them.

I felt so sad I wanted to ride after Nora and just keep going, leaving Pa and Ma behind. But I knew I couldn't.

"You'll see her again, Son," Pa said and I looked at him.

"You think so?" I was surprised that he had said such a thing. I didn't think it was in him to show any tenderness.

"God willing," he said.

By then, Leon and Nora were out of sight and I felt empty inside, all torn up at the parting. But when I looked back at Pa, I felt a tiny ray of hope just glimmering like a spark in the back of my mind.

And I missed Nora something fierce, even before she had actually left to go north with her folks. At that moment, I was sure I couldn't live without her, and after Pa walked away, I almost cried.

5

AFTER A FRETFUL NIGHT OF TOSSING AND TURNING SO MUCH that my bed the next morning looked as if someone had been murdered in it, I decided to ride over to the Carrero ranch and see Nora. Just thinking about her leaving was like getting hit with a twenty-pound sledgehammer. My mind was a jumble of thoughts, and even though I had stayed up late, reading and writing in my journal, I couldn't get Nora out of my mind. And, she was in my dreams, too, although in a different form and with a different face. I was bathed in sweat when I woke up and my nightshirt was a soggy mass of misshapen cloth.

Dawn was breaking when I got out of my bunk, but it was still dark inside my room. I stubbed my toe on a chair while walking toward the wardrobe where my clothes hung.

"You're up mighty early," Luke said.

His voice startled me and I must have jumped a foot inside my skin.

"I-I'm going to ride over to Leon Carrero's ranch before it gets too hot."

Luke stirred on his bunk and I could see his lanky body rising to a sitting position. His feet swung over the edge of the bed.

"Who were you wrasslin' with last night?"

I laughed. "I couldn't sleep."

"That makes two of us."

"Sorry. I can't get over the Carreros leaving."

"Nora," he said.

"Yes, Nora."

I heard Luke pick up his shirt and fish in one of the pockets for his makings. A rustle of cloth and the faint crackle of cigarette paper. Light seeped through the window, outlining one side of his face. The side window faced south, was the first to catch the rising sun. The back window faced west and gave me my sunsets when I was inside, like a constantly changing painting every evening.

"You've been sweet on that gal for a long time," Luke said.

"Long enough that I don't want to lose her."

"But she's leaving."

"Yes."

"You'll pine for her, but you'll get over it. People come and go in life."

"No, I won't get over it, Luke."

"What's all that writing you do at night? Love letters?"

I felt my face flush, but I knew Luke couldn't see me. I went to the cabinet and got down my clothes, which were hanging on a dowel. I slipped into my shirt and pants, then went over to my bed and roved beneath it for my boots. I slipped them on. A match flared and Luke lit his quirly. The match went out and I was temporarily blinded from looking at it when it was aflame.

"No, it's just a journal I keep."

"A journal? Like a diary?"

"Sort of. I've been writing in it ever since Ma bought

me a little bound book and taught me to read and write. I have about a dozen of them, I guess."

"What for?"

I had to think about that for a moment or two. When I started writing in the journals, it was just a way to practice my handwriting. Then I started thinking about what was happening around me and began writing down little phrases about those events. Later, after reading *The Iliad* and *The Odyssey*, I realized how powerful words were, the power of language itself. And, I began to look for that magic and power in my own writing. And I felt that power when I put thought to what I was writing down in my journal. As if everything I was doing was worthwhile. I kept the journals in a locked strongbox, because I didn't want my folks reading them. They might not like all of my observations. There were things in there about Barney and Luke, too, and about Nora, the Comanches. So, the journals became a kind of record of my life and the lives of others close to me.

"I don't know," I told Luke. "I guess it's just a way to make sense of things that happen. Writing gives me a chance to think things out."

"Good enough," Luke said. "I wish I could write."

"You can't write?"

"Nope. Not even my name."

"I could teach you, Luke."

"Too late for that. 'Sides, I don't really have nothin' to say that's worth puttin' on paper."

"I'll bet you do."

Luke got up and walked out the back door. I lit a lamp and got out my razor, shaved my face. I threw the dirty water out and filled the porcelain bowl for Luke, who was working on his second cigarette by the time I was ready to go to the barn.

"Tell Ma I'll be home for supper, will you?"

"Sure, Chip. You ride easy, hear?"

In a half hour, I was heading for the Carrero ranch, which was about eight miles away as the crow flies. I had my Winchester with me, and my Colt .44, but wasn't expecting any trouble. The sun was up and it was a beautiful day, still cool, with soft shadows puddled under the brush and the meadowlarks singing, the quail piping in the distance. It felt good to see the land come alive as the sun rose in the sky. There were small animal and bird tracks everywhere, and I jumped jackrabbits every so often, which kept my horse awake.

Leon was outside the house, loading up one of the wagons. Seeing him put a chair on top of the pile of goods gave me a sickening feeling. Nora and Kathleen were putting sacks and valises in another wagon, both walking in and out of the house, trudging up the steps of the porch as if they were carrying a heavy burden even though their hands were empty on the return trip.

"Chip, you come to help?" Leon asked.

"Sure, I'll help, Leon."

"We pretty much got it. But you can help me hitch up the horses."

I saw the two Mexican wranglers who worked for Leon driving cattle up the long valley toward the house. It all seemed so unreal that I sat there on my horse for a long moment, stunned that the Carreros were really packing up and leaving.

I dismounted, wrapped my reins around the hitchrail in front of the yard.

Nora waved to me the next time she came out of the house and I waved back. Her mother seemed bent on ignoring me. Leon finished tying down his load and stepped back from the wagon.

"You leaving today?" I asked him.

"As soon as we hitch up the horses."

"I wanted to talk to Nora before you go."

"Sure. Go on. If I need you, I'll give a holler."

Nora was packing the last of their pots into the back of the wagon when I walked over to her. Her mother was stuffing a fry pan in one corner of the wagon.

"There," Kathleen said. "All the cooking utensils are in the back of the wagon, within easy reach. I think that's it, Nora."

"Hello, Mrs. Carrero," I said.

"Chip."

"I hate to see you leave."

"Your family should be leaving with us, if you want my advice."

"Yes'm."

"Nora, your father's in a hurry. If you're going to say good-bye to Chip, make it quick so we can be on our way. I'm sorry, Chip, to be so short with you, but we are fearful of lingering. One of the hands saw unshod pony tracks this morning."

My blood chilled.

Before I could say anything, Nora grabbed my hand and led me away. We walked around to the back of the house where we could be alone.

"Chip, if you really love me, you'll come with us," Nora said, whirling to face me as soon as she had stopped. Her words caught me by surprise, as did the expression on her face.

"Huh?"

"You heard me. If your family refuses to face up to the danger, that's no concern of yours. You're a man. You can make your own decisions."

"Nora, I can't abandon my father and mother."

Her eyes flashed. She spread her legs and put her balled up fists on her hips. She was delivering an ultimatum. It was obvious to me that she had given a lot of thought to what she was saying.

"It seems to me," she said, "that your mother and father

are putting you in danger by staying at your ranch. They know the Comanches are coming. They know what happened to the Long family. If you want to live, you'll make up your own mind and come with us. If you care for me, Chip, you'll leave."

"Nora, I care for you. I really love you. But I can't just pick up and leave. I couldn't do a thing like that to my folks."

She turned her back on me and folded her arms across her chest in an attitude of defiance.

"Then good-bye, Chip. I have nothing else to say to you. I don't care if I never see you again."

I grabbed her shoulders and spun her around. I looked into her sparkling blue eyes. I could see the anger in them. Her lips were compressed into a hard line. It was as if all her love had turned suddenly to hate. But there was something else, too. Something in her eyes that made me cringe inside. A look of contempt.

"Nora, don't shut me out of your life over this. If you love me, you'll wait for me. I think we'll leave here one of these days. But not right now."

"It's now or never," she spat, and knocked my hands away from her shoulders. "You come with me now, or I never want to see you again."

Her words were like a slap across my face.

"Your mother told you to do this, didn't she?" I asked.

Then Nora did slap me.

"How dare you bring my mother into this, Chip. No, she did not. We're leaving. Now. And, I don't want to worry whether or not you'll be killed or scalped. So, if you don't come with us, I'll just put you out of my mind. Forever."

I didn't want it to end like this. I cared very deeply for Nora. I thought she was being unreasonable, that this was not the time to deliver an ultimatum. She was overwrought, I was sure. The moving, the unsettling feeling of being uprooted must have addled her mind.

"Nora, please listen to reason. I can't go with you. I just can't. And, if you really cared for me, or for my folks, you wouldn't ask me to just walk away from them. They're my own flesh and blood."

"And I'm not," she said, her words lashing out at me like steel-studded whips. "Good-bye, Chip. I hope you come to your senses one day."

Before I could stop her, she started running. She ran around to the front of the house. I walked out there behind her.

She stood with both her parents. All three of them were glaring at me.

"Chip, you'd better ride on back home," Leon said. "You've worn out your welcome here."

The horses were hitched to the wagons. Their dog, which had been roaming somewhere when I rode up, was running around in circles, barking.

"Leon, you know I can't just . . ."

"Chip," Kathleen said, "just leave. Now. Nora has said all that she has to say."

They turned away from me then. Nora climbed up on one wagon with her father, while Kathleen got atop the seat of the other one, with their dog, Mose. Leon loosened the brake and the wagon started to move. He snapped the reins over the backs of the four horses.

Nora didn't even look back when the wagon rolled away from me. I crumpled up inside, fought back the tears welling up in my eyes.

The cattle moved out behind the two wagons. I could hear the Mexicans yelling and see them riding on both flanks, waving their serapes like bullfighting capes. The wagons were swallowed up in the cloud of dust raised by the nearly one hundred head of cattle that were on the move.

There was a bitter taste in my mouth. I wondered if Nora

really meant what she had said, that she would forget about me and never wanted to see me again.

I walked to my horse and unwrapped the reins. I looked at the deserted house, the front door open, gaping on an empty room. It seemed that I could see shadows moving around inside and hear muffled conversations. But it was only the wind whispering through the vacant rooms.

I climbed up on the saddle and turned toward home. I was all broken up inside, and I was crying like a little baby.

"Nora," I murmured. "I love you."

The sound of my voice only made me feel more lonesome and I kept on crying because I couldn't stop feeling sorry for myself and for Nora.

6

MA SAW ME RIDE UP AFTER I RETURNED FROM THE NOW DE-
serted Carrero ranch. She was hanging wet clothes on the
line out back on a rope strung between two small poplars.
The wind was whipping the clothes, making them flap like
white and blue banners.

"You're back early," she said. "Did you see Nora?"

"I don't want to talk about it, Ma."

"Well, you will talk about it, Chip. If it's that bad. You
know how I feel about keeping things inside of you. Bad
things."

"She's gone. All of them are gone. Cattle, horses, furniture. Everything."

"So, you're sad. Maybe you'll see her again one day."

She picked up her empty basket and started toward the
house, one hand pushing her hair aside so that the blowing
strands didn't sting her eyes.

"She never wants to see me again."

Ma stopped and looked at me. Her eyes scanned my

face and it was like being under a powerful magnifying glass. Ma didn't miss much.

"You've been crying, Chip. Your face is streaked."

"I know. I couldn't help it."

She set down the laundry basket and hugged me. But I was through crying. I was through feeling sorry for myself.

"She wanted you to go with her, didn't she?"

"Yeah, Ma, she did."

"You could have gone with her."

"If I were that selfish, maybe."

"Or thoughtless."

She didn't come right out and say it, but I knew she was talking about Nora. That it was thoughtless of her to ask me to just walk away from Ma and Pa. She wouldn't have done it.

"I miss her, Ma."

"I know. Sometimes it takes a great deal of courage to do what you did."

"I don't know what courage is, Ma. I didn't feel brave or courageous. I just didn't want to do what she asked me to. I wouldn't want to hurt you and Pa."

"No, but the courage was there. You not only hurt her, you hurt yourself. But you did what your heart told you to do. You listened to your own conscience and faced up to a hard decision. You made a decision to let her go and that took great courage, my son."

"Thanks, Ma."

"I'm glad you had sense enough to say no to Nora. Sometimes it's easier to follow the crowd, but the man who forges his own path is better off. It's not easy, but in the long run, you will benefit by your decision."

"I hope you're right, Ma. I wanted to go with them. But I knew it wouldn't be right."

"Then you have a conscience, Chip. That's good." She laughed and picked up the basket again. "Now, you'd better find your father and Luke. I think they're in the barn doing something. Probably waiting for me to call them to lunch."

I found Luke and Pa in the barn, as Ma had said, and they were both sitting down working on harness, checking all the lines and yokes and blinders. I wondered why.

"Just in case," Pa said.

"In case of what?"

Pa looked at Luke. Luke, wisely perhaps, kept his silence. He was rubbing Neat's Foot Oil on one of the reins, slicking it down so that it was limber and pliant and shining like a new piece of leather.

"Leon pulled out, didn't he? We saw the dust."

"Yeah. They all left."

"We might not be far behind," Pa said.

I sat down and grabbed a mass of tangled harness and started to pull the lines free of the knots. My heart seemed to skip a beat.

"Did Ma change her mind?" I asked.

"Not yet, but she will."

"What makes you think that, Pa?"

"This morning, after you left, she come and talked to me about leavin'."

"What did she say?"

Pa looked up from the traces in his hand and a peculiar look came over his face, as if he was coming up from some deep dark place way down inside him. His eyes shone like agates as a shaft of sunlight striped his face. Little motes of dust danced in the shining ray as if it was some living thing come down from heaven.

"She told me that she would miss the Palo Duro if we had to leave. She said she knew we would have to go one of these days. She said she wouldn't be able to stand you pinin' your heart out for Nora."

I was so choked up, I couldn't say anything. My father

turned his head and his face went into shadow as if he had suddenly donned a dark mask.

"She said let the goddamned Comanches have the place, that they would not have our blood."

"Ma said that?"

"Ever' word," Pa said.

I sat there stunned. It was not like Ma to curse, except when she was very mad.

"What about you, Luke?" I asked. "Are you coming with us?"

Luke kept on oiling the leather in his lap.

"Naw, I'm goin' to stay on here and let Red Hand rip my scalp off so's his kids can have a plaything."

I grinned.

"When do we leave, Pa?"

"Not right soon, maybe. I'm just gettin' ready. You just have to have patience, Son."

I untangled more tack and wondered if I would have the patience to wait until Ma was ready. I kept thinking of Nora, already setting off for new country. I wanted to chase after her and tell her we were coming, not to be in any hurry.

For some reason I recalled the first time Nora and I had made love. We had taken a picnic lunch with us one morning before anyone was awake and ridden off to a creek we knew where there were some shade trees and grass. She had brought some light blankets to sit on and we spread these beneath the trees. We talked and listened to the music of the creek and then we kissed. I held her close in my arms and she pulled me even tighter against her so that I felt her breasts pressing into my chest. Our kisses became more fervent and fevered and then we were undressing each other, both of us bewildered by what was happening. She said she wanted me and I told her I wanted her.

We were so young and inexperienced, but the mystery

was there, beckoning to us, and we coupled and found our way. In that moment, I believe, Nora became a woman, and I know I became a man. We followed our desires to the very pinnacle of the world and beyond, to heaven. We soared with eagles and we floated with angels high above the earth. I fell in love with her then and I have loved her ever since. That deep mystery of her haunted me now, pervaded my thoughts and I wished we were lying on a blanket by that creek now with the wind tousling her auburn hair and flicking soft music from the waters lapping against the bank.

"Hear that?" Pa said, jarring me from my reverie.

"What?" I said, without thinking.

"I damned sure hear it," Luke said. "Grab your rifles. That's a damned Comanche."

I heard it then, a high-pitched yelping sound that sent shivers up my spine.

All I had was my six-gun. Pa picked up his rifle by the barn door where it had been leaning up against the wall. Luke reached back and grabbed his from inside a stall. We all raced out of the barn. I looked around for Ma, but didn't see her. She was my first thought, and I dreaded that she might be in danger.

"Where is the bastard?" Pa asked as we split up and ran out toward the road.

"Yonder," Luke said, pointing. "It's a Mexican bein' chased by a pair of 'em."

The Mexican was riding hard down our lane. He was leaning forward over the saddle, hugging the pommel for dear life. Behind him, two Comanches, or two Indians, were riding after him, screeching in their high-pitched voices.

Luke dropped to one knee and jacked a shell into the chamber of his big Henry Yellow Boy. I saw him lead the closest Indian and then squeeze off a shot. His rifle barked.

Smoke and flame spewed from the barrel and I heard the whistle of the bullet.

A second later, the lead Indian seemed to twitch as the bullet caught him in the chest. He threw up his arms and his rifle went flying. His pony ran out from under him.

Pa shot at the second Indian and missed. He levered another shell into the chamber and put the barrel behind the Indian and swung in front of him. As the Indian disappeared behind the muzzle, Pa squeezed the trigger. White smoke billowed from his barrel and a stream of orange sparks belched from the muzzle. The bullet hit the Indian in the side. The brave twisted in the saddle as his rifle slipped from his fingers, hit the ground, and danced on its stock before it upended and fell flat.

The Mexican was whipping his horse and spurring it, as he dashed straight toward me. I held up my hands, one of them with my pistol in it, in a signal to stop. I could see his face. The man was terrified, and I recognized him, even so. He was covered with blood and I knew he had been shot. He reined his horse to a halt and the animal skidded sideways, raising a curtain of dust beneath its belly.

"Any more?" Pa shouted, as Ma came running out of the house with a rifle in her hands.

"Don't see none," Luke said. "Let's go check 'em."

Ma started toward me as the Mexican toppled from the saddle. I ran up and grabbed him as he fell. Blood soaked through his shirt and onto me.

"Why, isn't that one of Leon's vaqueros?" Ma said.

"It's Juan Gallegos, Ma. He was driving Leon's cattle this morning."

"Oh my," she said, as she lay her rifle down and bent over the wounded drover. "Juan, can you hear me?"

Juan's eyelids fluttered and then his eyes stayed open. They were glazed with pain. There was blood rimming his

mouth and when Ma pulled at his shirt, exposing his bare
chest, I saw an ugly black hole just above his abdomen.
Little slivers of bone jutted out from the edges of the hole.
Blood pumped through the wound with every hard breath
he took.

"Lie still," Ma said. "Chip, go fetch him some water."

I ran to get a pail of water from the pump while Ma
tended to Gallegos. My heart was pounding with excitement. Out of the corner of my eye, I saw Pa and Luke staring down at the closest Indian, the one that Luke had shot.
Pa lifted something from the Indian's sash, but I couldn't
tell what it was.

"*Muchos Indios*," Gallegos was saying when I returned
with the water.

"*Calmate*, Juan," my mother said in Spanish. "You must
lie still. Do you have thirst? I will try and stop the bleeding."

"Much blood," Gallegos said. "It hurts very much."

"I know. I'm going to wash your wound and see if I
can . . . Chip, have you a knife on you?"

I drew my knife, handed it to my mother. She set the
knife down beside Gallegos and picked up the pail of water. She held it over his wound and poured some into the
hole and around it. She cut off part of her dress and began
to wash the wound, very gently. Even so, Gallegos winced
when the water hit the hole in his body. There was a terrible stench coming from the wound.

"The bullet ruptured some of his intestines," Ma said. "I
fear Juan needs a surgeon. But I will do what I can for
him."

"What happened, Juan?" I asked, squatting down next
to my mother. "I need to know about Nora."

"They attack us," he said. "Many Comanches. They had
rifles. They shoot Pedro Morales and I ride for help when
Leon, he tell me to come here."

"Chip, he shouldn't talk," Ma said.

"I need to know about Nora."

"This man's life is hanging by a thread."

Ma washed his wound and then stuck her finger inside, probing for the bullet or lead ball. Gallegos tensed and tears streamed from his eyes. He seemed to be in a great deal of pain and the probing made it worse.

I looked up and saw my father and Luke walking over to the Comanche Pa had shot. They both knelt down to examine the body. It seemed they were taking hours, when I knew we should be riding to help the Carrero family.

"Ma, we should be going to help Leon."

"Wait for your father, Chip." She bent over Gallegos and listened to his breathing. The man did not look good. His eyes were glazed and his breathing was labored, as if every breath might be his last.

"Juan," my mother said, "there is a lead ball inside you. I can just feel it. I can't work it out without cutting you open. Do you understand?"

"I am dead," Gallegos said.

"No, you are alive, but only a surgeon can help you. If I try and cut the lead out, you could bleed to death. Understand?"

"I understand," he said.

"I'm going to pack the wound and we will try and take you to Amarillo in the wagon."

"No," Gallegos said. "Too far. I bleed much. Inside."

"How many Comanches came at you, Mr. Gallegos?" I asked.

"I think five, or six, maybe."

"That would leave three or four," I said. "Maybe Leon was able to kill the others, or drive them off."

Gallegos closed his eyes and winced from a sudden pain.

Ma put the cloth over the wound, but I noticed she didn't try and stuff it inside to stop the bleeding. As if she knew Gallegos was dying and that there was nothing she could do to save him.

"Maybe you wish to pray, Juan," she said.

He was too weak to cross himself, but he murmured some words in Spanish and I heard the words *padre* and *Cristo*. Then his voice faded away. His breathing got worse. It sounded as if he was trying to take in air with a piece of paper over his mouth. Then the sound went into his throat and he choked, then gasped. Blood spewed from his mouth as he convulsed. His eyes rolled back in their sockets and then all the light went out of them. He made a final gasp and then lay stiff and still.

"He's gone," Ma said. "Lord have mercy."

I thought that was an ironic statement since my mother's name is Mercy. But it also seemed fitting. Ma pushed his eyelids down so that Gallegos wasn't staring up at her with those now sightless eyes.

Pa and Luke came up then, and looked down at the dead man.

"Too bad," Pa said. "Those two Comanches are dead."

"Pa, we've got to go help Leon. Gallegos said there were only five or six Comanches who attacked them. Maybe . . ."

Luke stepped up closer. He had something in his hand. My heart lurched when I saw the scalp. It was bloody, but it also had a reddish hue.

"I found this on one of them bucks," Luke said. "It don't look good."

Mother let out a cry and her hands flew to her mouth. She cringed at the sight of the bloody hair. I stood up and stared at it, thoughts of Nora swirling through my mind. My stomach roiled with bile and I felt sick. I gulped in air and fought back the queasiness.

"Pa," I said.

"Chip, it may not be . . ."

But my eyes filled with sudden tears and I clenched my fists in anger.

At that moment, I wanted to kill the nearest Comanche. At the same time, I hated myself for not going with Leon and his family. My world had turned dark with guilt and regret as if a black cloud had slid across the face of the sun, turning day into night.

7

"IT AIN'T HERS," LUKE SAID.

"What?"

"This ain't Nora's hair. It's her mama's, Chip."

"How-how do you know?" I asked.

"It's an older woman's hair and it's not soft as Nora's. Wrong color, too."

Luke held out the strands of long reddish hair and I looked at the clump more closely. He was right. It was not Nora's hair. It was her mother's.

"That's Kathleen's hair," Ma said. "Oh, how terrible. That poor woman."

"Well, are we going to stand around here and blubber all day?" Pa said. "Those folks need help, and we'd better start wearin' out horses gettin' over to 'em."

"Damned right," Luke said. "I'll saddle up your horse, Keith."

"Mine, too," Ma said. "I'll just run inside and get more ammunition for my rifle."

We followed the tracks of Gallegos and the two

Comanches backward until we came upon signs of where the Indians started drawing blood from the Carreros. We passed a dead cow, its mouth gaping open, black tongue lolling out to one side, flies boiling at its dead eyes.

Then we began to see items that had fallen off the wagons: a chair, a porcelain bowl, a vase, a slop jar, linens, clothes and such.

These were sickening things to see, all scattered over the ground like that. As if the Carrero house had been struck by a whirlwind, gutted out by a twister and the people carried far away.

Pa gestured for us to spread out and we continued north, following the tracks and the trail of debris. The trail was easy to follow, and my heart tugged every time I saw unshod pony tracks, but I kept staring ahead, looking for the wagons, expecting to hear Nora's voice calling to me at any moment; expecting to see her waving to me from atop her wagon seat.

Then, on the horizon, a dreaded sight appeared: a circus of buzzards wheeling in the sky on invisible and silent carousels. We began to see lone cattle standing as if stunned, lost, bewildered. The tracks were all moiled and thick on the trail, dirt dug up from running hooves and spoor splayed out everywhere, in all directions, as if something horrible scattered the herd, or caused it to stampede.

Luke ranged far ahead to my right, while Pa and Ma rode gingerly on my left, as if afraid to venture forward with too great a speed, fearful of what they might find.

More flotsam, then, detritus fallen from the wagons I had seen the family loading that morning, and each piece of furniture or kitchenware carried its own dire message and each one threaded with the feeling of great havoc. My stomach churned and my temples throbbed with the ghastly and audible pounding of my heart.

Then Luke rode up on the first wagon and I put my

horse into a gallop. My folks saw me fly by and spurred their horses into a trot, then a run, and the three of us arrived at the wagon as witnesses to a horror none of us could have imagined.

"That's . . . oh, my God," my mother exclaimed, "Kathleen, isn't it?"

"That's the missus," Luke said, his voice deep and resonant, as if issuing from some deep and cavernous tomb. "God rest her soul."

Kathleen Carrero lay on her back, spread-eagled like a broken rag doll, only a shred of her dress remaining in tatters under her arms and, like some bloody scarf, around her throat.

Ma gasped and my father choked on something in his throat. Luke turned away from the hideous sight and looked north toward the horizon. I followed his gaze and saw the other wagon, asprawl like some broken toy, less than five hundred yards away, the horses gone, the wagon tongue slanted toward the ground as if it had been run there by some terrible force. And, next to the wagon, a clutch of claws and beaks and flapping wings as buzzards hopped and fought over something dark and still lying on the ground.

"Christ," Luke said in a breathy curse that might have been a prayer under other circumstances.

"What?" I said, not wanting any answer.

"This warn't done by no five Comanches," Luke said. "They must have had a passel of 'em come up later after running Gallegos off."

"We'd better go see what that is on the ground by that other wagon," Pa said, as if summoning up the courage to ride over to it.

"I'll stay here," Ma said. "Maybe I can cover Kathleen, give her some little amount of dignity."

I followed Pa and Luke numbly up to the other wagon. It was obvious that the Comanches had taken things from both, but I wasn't taking an inventory. I was trying to pull out of the shock I felt at seeing such a change in the wagons from that morning. Everything had been so neatly packed away and tied down and now there was just a shambles all around, with personal items scattered and strewn with no regard to their intrinsic value to the Carrero family.

Luke shooed off the buzzards that were ripping and tearing into Leon's body. He was lying face down, but there were bullet holes in his shirt and pants. Part of his scalp had been cut and the hair ripped off leaving what looked like a huge wet scab, with all those hair holes looking like red pin pricks. Luke slid out of the saddle and turned Leon's body over and there was dirt and grass stuffed into his mouth, which had been slit wider at the two corners. I nearly threw up at the sight of that mouth, but I closed my eyes and tried to think of how Leon had looked that morning, his expression dour and fixed. This didn't even look like Mr. Carrero. It looked like something made out of wax and dirt and blood. One of his eyes had been plucked out by the buzzards and that made his face look even more distorted than it was.

Luke took the name of the Lord in vain once again.

Pa got sick. He leaned over and threw up all over the ground, splattering his horse's front legs.

Like a damned fool, I rode up and looked inside the wagon. The Comanches had taken most of the stuff that had been in it, including the pots and pans, some of the clothes. I thought they had left a pile of clothes in one corner, but when I looked more closely, I saw that more than clothing lay in a heap. Sick to my stomach, I climbed out of the saddle and stepped down into the wagon bed. I grabbed the clothes and felt something underneath, something soft and yielding. Then I saw her, all doubled up into a ball, scalped and ravaged almost beyond recognition.

It was Nora and it broke my heart to see what was left

of her. Both her arms were broken and her legs bore large ugly bruises. Her face was smashed in, so that her beauty had vanished into a hideous mask of blood and bone and broken teeth. I recoiled in horror and then felt ashamed of myself. My revulsion turned to pity and I began to sob as I looked at what Red Hand had done to my beautiful Nora.

There was very little that was human left of her. I could not fathom how terrible her last moments of life must have been. Nor could I understand how another human could be filled with such hatred and cruelty as to crush such a lovely flower and grind it underfoot as if it had no value. My grief was enormous and I covered the two large wounds on her chest where her young breasts had been.

I cursed and cried until Luke pulled me away from Nora's mutilated corpse. I had lost all track of time and place, so deep was my grief. He covered her up and got me out of the wagon, held onto me while I shook all over with the torment that raked my very soul.

"I loved her, Luke," I cried and he patted the back of my head.

"I know, Chip."

Then Pa was there, and I looked up at his face and saw his eyes flicker with compassion and understanding. I had never seen such a look on his face before, nor had I seen such strength in his visage, the granite jaw, the tightly compressed lips, the stern and noble cast to his expression.

"My son," he said. "It's so sad. She was a lovely girl."

"She-she was a woman, Pa."

"I know. Yes, she was. Come with me. Your mother can give you comfort."

Later, Luke and Pa found two shovels in one of Leon's wagons and we buried the dead. Ma and I wept when we covered those people with dirt and rocks, but Pa and Luke remained stoic and pensive. Pa said some words over the graves, but I wasn't listening to him. I was thinking of Nora, the way she had been, smiling, laughing, full of life. I recalled little moments between us, the kisses, the caresses, the tender and sweet lovemaking under the stars on summer nights. I tried not to think of her broken body lying cold in the ground, her remains wrapped in a pink pastel sheet that had once adorned her bed.

Afterward, Ma drew Pa to her side with a private look. Luke and I watched her to see what she would say.

"This changes everything, Keith," Ma said. "You were right. We can't stay here anymore. There is too much blood, too much death."

"Leon tried to take too many things with him," Pa said. "We won't make the same mistake."

"No, we won't. We'll take only what we need to get by. The furniture will stay. We'll buy or make what we need when we get to our new home."

"We have to take the cattle."

"Only as many as you, Luke, and Chip can drive that far."

"And the horses, of course."

"Foodstuffs, cooking utensils. One wagon. All the rest stays behind," she said.

Pa sighed and looked at Luke, who nodded.

I felt better, knowing that Luke was going with us, and I thought of what I would take. My books, my guns, and my clothes. That was all I needed. Plenty of ammunition.

We looked for the other drover but did not find him. His name was Pedro Morales. Luke found a place with a lot of blood and some strange markings on the ground. This was next to a dead cow.

"Pedro made his last stand here," Luke said. "And then they killed him and dragged his body somewhere."

"Do you think he might still be alive?" Pa asked.

Luke shook his head. "Too much blood. But maybe."

"Should we try and find him?" Ma asked.

"I think we should pack up and get the hell out of here," Luke said.

Ma and Pa agreed, and so did I.

So we did not follow the drag marks to find out what had happened to Pedro.

But the tracks followed us.

We found the body of Pedro Morales, scalped and broken, his mouth stuffed full of dirt and grass, on our front porch.

His clothes had been worn off from the rough ground over which he had been dragged.

"He was alive until he got here," Luke said.

"How do you know?" I asked.

"Look at his fingers. There's dirt under the nails where he tried to stop from being drug, and look at his boots. He dug in his heels, too, wore 'em off at the ends. They waited until they got him here and then they killed him. Real slow."

"What savages," Pa said. "It makes my blood boil."

And, more ominous, on our front door, plain as the burning day, a bloody handprint.

Red Hand, we knew, would come back here. And, when he did, he would kill and butcher us all.

8

LUKE AND I DID MOST OF THE CULLING WHEN WE PUT TO-gether the herd we would drive to Jefferson Territory. We cut out all the calves and their mothers, except for the hardiest ones. We kept the hardiest Hereford bulls and the strong cows which had not come fresh yet. It was tough to pare down our stock to just forty-five head, but that's what we did, while Pa helped Ma load the single wagon we would take with us. I knew that Ma was feeling badly about leaving behind so many of her things, but she packed without complaint. We took along tools, cooking utensils, a few pewter plates, those things most durable, most needed.

Luke and I buried the two Mexican drovers under a live oak tree atop a little knoll and I spoke the words over them, feeling empty inside and still mourning for Nora.

"Sorry, God," I said. "We couldn't bury Mose because we couldn't find him. Luke said it was likely he was being eaten for supper tonight, so we ask that you take him in, too. He's a real good dog. Amen."

Pa was pretty smart. We set out north, but he devised a

zigzag route that avoided any main roads or followed creeks where we left no tracks. We managed to elude any Comanches that might have been following us. We kept a tight formation, our rifles at the ready, with the wagon in the center of the small herd that followed the leader Luke had selected. We did not hurry, and we took turns standing guard at night, with two of us awake at all times.

Ma and I stood our watches together and took turns singing to the cattle we had bedded down for the night. Luke and Pa took the first watch after supper and woke up Ma and me after midnight.

After supper every night, Ma would have me read to everyone from one of my books. I read *The Vicar of Wakefield,* which Ma and I liked, and then started reading *The Decameron* by an Italian named Boccaccio. Luke liked the stories in that book a lot. Once or twice, I noticed my mother blushing by the firelight, and once she and Pa exchanged funny looks at each other at the end of one very bawdy story. Sometimes I'd read a play by Shakespeare and change my voice for the different characters. This made everyone laugh, much to my embarrassment.

Just before nearly every dawn, we heard the coyotes singing in the distance and we rode around the herd crooning and talking to them so that they never once stampeded. We saw to it that the cows grazed every day and had plenty of water.

Still, it was a long and arduous journey, up through flat, treeless Kansas and then westward to the Territory over desolate land that was new to us. We began to see the country change, with little buttes appearing on the horizon and then larger ones. The vistas each day were wondrous and magnificent, but it was tougher to find water and often we had to drift off course to find grass. For a time we followed old buffalo trails that were like wide swaths cutting through broken country, and we watched the buttes and mesas for hostile Indians, expecting warriors to appear at any moment and swoop down on us.

I noticed, from time to time, that Pa kept digging out a sheaf of papers and studying them. One day, I asked him what they were.

"Maps that Leon gave me. And some names of friends of his."

"Leon gave you maps to the Territory?"

"Yes. He said he felt sure that we'd follow him out one day."

"Looks like he was right." Pa showed me the maps, which were very crudely drawn, but they had landmarks sketched on them, along with rivers and creeks and compass directions.

"Mostly, I follow the stars," Pa said. "I take our bearings every night and follow the sun during the day. We're doing pretty well, I'd say."

"How come you never told me or Ma about these maps?"

"Sometimes it's best not to make known your intentions."

"That's a little bit like lying, isn't it, Pa?"

"Maybe. I like to think of it as being kind to your mother. She worries a lot, you know."

"She doesn't worry any more than any of us, far as I can see."

"Well, she's stubborn."

"Maybe not as stubborn as you, Pa."

He winked and smiled at me, but Ma had known about the maps all along, ever since Leon had given them to Pa. She just never let on and allowed Pa to keep his secret.

The huge mesas and buttes gave way to flat prairie with lots of grass and plenty of water. Sometimes, the cattle would be wading through grass up to their bellies, and they grew fat on the land. We had lost only one calf by the time we came in sight of the mountains. But we lost three grown cows. One got its leg caught in a gopher hole, and Luke had to shoot it. We didn't waste the meat. Another was brought down by wolves during the night and there wasn't much left of it by morning. A third wandered off and went down into a gulley during a rainstorm and was carried away by a wall of water in a flash flood.

Pa told Luke that he was grateful to him that we hadn't lost much on the trail and he credited Luke with that. We kept the herd tight and Luke was mainly responsible for the herding. I think the cattle looked at him as their leader more than they did the bull that was always out front. A rattlesnake bit that little calf on the leg, which swelled up and pussed and finally killed the little heifer. It was good eating, though, and a welcome change from antelope and jackrabbit. We didn't see any buffalo, but Luke shot several antelope, picking out the younger ones which had the most tender meat. He told us they tasted something like goat, and I asked him where he had eaten goat before.

"When I was growin' up, we was poor," he said, "and so we ate goat, them we wasn't milkin'."

The day before, we had seen some Indians in the distance. I noticed Ma's face drain of color, and Pa's lips tighten. I also noticed the darting little shadows of fear in his eyes. But, Luke now, he just rode easy and let one hand droop over the stock of his rifle, and his eyes were chips of flint, hard as agate.

"Luke," I said, "what's courage?"

"Courage? Never thought about it much."

"I need to know."

"Why?"

"Just in case I ever need it."

Luke laughed.

"I reckon it's just something that follows on the coattails of fear."

"Explain that, will you, Luke?"

"I mean, when you run out of fear, and maybe get mad enough, you get a shot of courage, like takin' a drink of whiskey when you're cold."

"So, it's not something you're born with."

"I reckon not. It's somethin' larnt."

"Learned from what?"

"Chip, you ask too many damned fool questions. You probably got your own kind of courage right inside you. When you need it, it'll be there."

"I hope so, Luke."

The land had a rhythm to it, and a sweet harmony. Some days I rode as if I was in a dream, my horse wading through an ocean of grass and the sky so blue it filled me with a wonder at all creation. And, it seemed to me, as we made that journey, that I became part of the land, and that the land became part of me. I felt at home and at peace. We slept on the ground at night, except Ma put down her good comforters, not mindful of how dirty they got, after Luke and I cleared away the rocks and made the ground smooth.

Out there, on the long prairie, I would look up at the stars and they seemed a lot closer than they did back home. They seemed bigger and brighter, and there was a kind of peace in that, too, as if, high above us, there was no war or killing or bad temper, just beauty floating out there in the pitch of night, stars winking down on us. The coyotes made music after the sun fell and the dark came on, pealing out ribbons of song that floated on the night air like some wilderness symphony. When they went silent, it was like being in a church after the choir had left. The music lingered in my mind and I knew that there was no other sound on earth exactly like it.

The land changed, too, as if by magic. Here and there we saw spires rising up like ancient towers, and grand buttes appear, like phalanxes of giant ships or structures that looked like buildings in the distance. We began to see prairie swifts darting through the air, and hunting hawks prowling the wind currents for small game. And always, there were the buzzards circling in the sky, their necks craning for any sign of death.

Then, one day, through the shimmering mirages and the haze, we saw the mountains, far in the distance. We were still some days away from them, but we could feel their immensity and power, like the great muscles of the earth, and we were drawn to them as if they meant safe haven. I was sorry that Nora wasn't there to see them, along with her family and the two Mexicans who had worked for them. As we drew closer, the mountains grew even larger and more majestic, and soon we saw white-capped peaks shining like beacons in the sun.

Pa kept looking at the maps and reading the stars at night. He told us we were right on course. We began to see more antelope and the coyotes kept us company at night, and we would occasionally see one or two during the day. And always, there was that great emptiness, that feeling of smallness and loneliness under that huge blue bowl of sky with its white flocks of clouds sailing toward us from the distant mountains.

We rode through a driving rain for two days. The rain blinded us and slowed us. The skies threw silver javelins at us, stinging our eyes and blinding us. We avoided the gullies and washes which roared with flash floods, and kept to high flat ground. When the rain stopped, finally, we looked up and saw the grandeur of the Rocky Mountains looming above the plain, the high peaks shining with mantles of snow, white as ermine.

As we drew closer to the mountains, we saw spirals of smoke, and then buildings.

"Pueblo," Pa said.

"Is that where we're going?" I asked.

"Nope. Just a stop to resupply and where I hope to meet a man who will guide us into the mountains."

"What man?"

"His name is Selva. Julio Selva. He was a friend of Leon Carrero's. A boyhood chum."

"How will you find this Selva?"

"He lives in an adobe south of town."

"An adobe? Like those in Texas?"

"Yeah. Just like them."

We circled Pueblo, seeing lots of activity, horse-drawn carts, dogs, cats, people walking, riding. We even saw some burros pulling wagons, or being ridden by young Mexicans and old ones with white beards.

Julio Selva lived on a patch of land that he said was sixteen hectares, some twenty acres or so, and he lived alone. He was a small, wiry man, whose face was lined and bronzed from the sun so that it looked like tanned leather. He saw all of our cattle and the wagon when it stopped in front of his small adobe. He came out, smoking a pipe.

"I see you have the longhorns with the white faces," he said. "You must be from *Tejas*."

"Texas, yes," Pa said. "My name is Keith Morgan."

"I am called Julio Selva."

"Yes, Leon Carrero told me about you."

"And how is Leon?"

"He is dead."

"*Que triste*. How very sad. How did he die?"

"Comanches." Pa told him the whole story after Julio invited us into his home where Pa made all the introductions.

"So, you want to take the cattle into the mountains. There is good grass there in the summertime. There is a place I told Leon about that would make a fine ranch. It is high in the mountains, and you must drive your cattle down to the flat in the winter."

"You will show us this place?" Pa asked.

"Yes, but it is very dangerous. Did you hear the news in Pueblo?"

"We did not stop in Pueblo," Ma said. "What news?"

"The army general, Custer, he was killed. Massacred, they say, by the Sioux and Cheyenne."

"Where?" Pa asked.

"Up north. In the Dakotas, I think. The people here think that this will give all of the tribes courage to attack the whites and drive them off their lands."

"Are there Sioux here?" Ma asked.

"No, there are no Sioux. The Southern Cheyenne used to come down this way, to Santa Fe and Taos. But I have not seen any in a long time. Maybe they will come."

"We left Texas because of the Comanches," Pa said. "We don't want to go anyplace where we might have to fight hostile Indians."

"This place," Selva said, "is very far back in the mountains, where the Rio Grande is a small creek in the summer. I think the Utes and the Arapahos do not go there anymore. And, if they do, you may be able to make friends with them."

"When can we go there?" Pa asked.

"Tomorrow. I will take you there. I have the deed to the land and I will sell it to you, if you like it there."

"We do not have much money," Ma said.

Selva laughed.

"The land is *muy barato,* very cheap. When you sell your cattle, you can pay me. First, you see if you like it there, eh?"

"We will talk it over tonight and let you know," Pa said.

"You may camp here and I will cook a fine supper for you tonight."

"You are not married?" Ma asked.

Selva shook his head and there was a look of sadness in his eyes.

"No. I am, how do you say, the widow?"

"A widower," Ma corrected.

"Yes. My wife and family all died."

"Oh, I'm sorry," Ma said. "How did they die?"

"The Utes killed them. But that was a long time ago."

"Where did this happen?" Ma asked, pressing Selva for more information.

"I will show you."

"You will show us? Was it around here?"

"Ah, no. It was in the place where we are going," Selva said, and I could see my mother draw back and a cloudiness come into her eyes. She looked at Pa, but he avoided her gaze. I looked over at Luke, who had said nothing the whole time we were inside Selva's house.

His eyebrows arched, but he said nothing.

Selva smiled as if he had said nothing to strike fear in our hearts.

I wondered what the hell we were getting into. And what kind of tribe were the Utes? Or the Arapaho, for that matter? It seemed to me that we were jumping from the frying pan right smack dab into the fire.

That night, Ma and Pa argued about going into the mountains and I never did hear the end of it because I fell asleep.

I dreamed of Nora and wild Indians and a soldier named Custer who had been massacred, so Selva told us, on a river called the Little Big Horn.

When I awoke in the morning, I asked myself where Selva was taking us, and the answer was to the same place where his family was massacred by the Utes.

But Ma said we were going with Selva after Pa, Luke, and Selva went into town for supplies, and I wondered what had changed her mind.

"We have to make a stand," she said. "We can't just keep wandering the earth. We're not Indians, you know."

"But what if the Utes attack us way up in those big mountains?" I said.

"Then we'll just have to deal with them, Chip. That's all. Once we're settled, I am not going to move again."

But I wasn't so sure. Ma had more courage than I had. I kept thinking of Custer and the Utes and I still had memories of the Comanches back in Texas, and all the people we knew who had been butchered by those savages.

It was late afternoon when we finally left Selva's and up into the green mountains. It would be many days e we reached our destination, and as soon as we left plain, I knew we were leaving behind all civilization d we might never see Pueblo again.

9

WE WOUND THROUGH THE MOUNTAINS, UP STEEP GRADES AND
through high passes, sometimes in single file. There was
plenty of grass for the cattle and horses and Selva did not
hurry. For me, it was like entering a strange new world, an
almost mythical kingdom of towering peaks, granite bluffs,
vast, lush valleys, and shining silver streams, some with
waterfalls cascading like fine-spun lace or crystal filigree.

As we climbed higher and higher, Ma got a headache and
had to take powders. Later, Pa, Luke, and I got headaches,
too, but they went away once we got used to the thin air.

Selva seemed at home in the high country and never
complained. He did not talk much, but just let us experience the country for ourselves. He could see the wonder in
our eyes, I'm sure, and I often saw him with a faint smile
on his face when we would all look up at a spectacular
snowcapped peak.

Finally, we wound along a wide stream over rocky
ground through a twisting valley. We emerged at a sloping
place with a log cabin, corrals, chutes, and other signs of

habitation. After seeing nothing but wilderness for days, the cabin was both a welcome and a startling sight. We were even more surprised when we saw horses and cows. A man and a woman stepped out onto the large porch and waved to us as we approached.

"This is Lost Creek," Selva explained. "It is part of the land you will own."

"But it looks like someone is living there," Ma said.

"That is Ruben Gonzalo, and his wife, Carmen," Selva said. "They keep the ranch supplied with meat and food, and care for the stock that is kept here. They are paid a small amount of money for this."

Four lively children burst through the front door and surrounded their parents, two boys and two girls. They looked healthy and their dark faces lit up with beaming smiles. This was obviously a happy family. I noticed cows in one of the lots, next to a fairly large barn. They were Guernseys.

"They sell the milk and butter," Selva said, when he saw me looking at the cows. "They also raise chickens and sell the eggs. When they have calves, those also, they sell. This is how they make the money, as well."

"Where do they sell all this?" I asked.

"There are some ranches not far from here, down along the way we came."

I had noticed no roads, but I wasn't looking for any. It was nice to know that we wouldn't be the only ones up here in this faraway place.

Beyond the cabin, grasslands sloped up to the small foothills, pristine and green as far as the eye could see. The creek ran through the property, glistening in the sunlight as if created by a master artist. The view of the grass and hills and towering mountains beyond was breathtaking and I drank it all in as if I were in some kind of dream while still wide awake.

Selva introduced us to Ruben Gonzalo and his wife, Carmen. Ruben ordered his children to go off and play, so we never heard their names.

"Ruben will guide you to the summer pastures," Selva said. "I will return in the month of September and help you bring the cattle down here for winter pasture."

"What about the property?" Pa asked. "How do we buy it from you?"

"Ruben has all the papers and will explain it to you. He is my agent."

Gonzalo smiled throughout this conversation and nodded. He was a stocky man, muscled, with a brooding mustache that gave him the look of a walrus. His eyes were small and deep set, and there were lines in his face that seemed to have been etched by many winters in the high country. His wife, Carmen, was a small stocky woman, with long black hair that was braided into a single strand that reached almost to her waist. She, too, was muscled, but she was very pretty and seemed amiable; she seemed not to speak much English, although I was sure she understood the language.

"We will go over the papers," Gonzalo said. "They are very simple. When Julio returns in September, you can pay him some little money."

"I would prefer to . . ."

"Keith," Ma said, "let's do it their way. See if we like the property before we sign any papers or pay out any money. Is that all right with you, Mr. Selva?"

"That is the way we should do it," Selva said. "You must build a cabin in that place where Gonzalo will take you. You will be very busy with the cattle and the building, but the logs are cut and the building will go quickly."

Pa was skeptical. As he later explained it, they might be building a cabin for Selva and he would back out of the transaction. Ma told him that they had to show a little trust and do business Selva's way. Until he showed that he was dishonest, they would have to trust him.

"And what of Gonzalo?" Pa asked.

"The same with him."

Selva rode back down the mountain and Gonzalo showed us where to quarter our herd. We put the horses up, grained and curried them.

"Tomorrow, we will go up into the mountains," Gonzalo said. "It is only a few miles."

Luke and I pastured our cattle, while Pa and Ma put up the horses and put the wagon beside the stables.

The air was thin, but fresh as a spring breeze, and truly invigorating after the hot weather down in Texas. Luke seemed to like the mountain air, too, because he kept gulping it in, and swelling out his chest.

"The cattle seem to be doing all right," I said, watching them take to grazing right off.

"Cattle don't get headaches."

"You got a headache?"

"Like my skull was split open with a broadax."

"I feel fine."

"You've got young blood, Chip. It ain't been trained to heavy air yet."

"Maybe I just don't believe in headaches. That's what women get all the time."

Luke didn't laugh, but I meant it as a joke.

"Well, maybe I don't have a real headache," he said. "It's probably just a broken skull."

"Why don't you ask Ma for some of her powders?"

"Naw, I reckon I'll just go someplace, lie down and die."

"Well, go ahead and suffer, then, Luke. I left all my sympathy back on the Palo Duro."

We walked back to the cabin and that evening I watched

a sunset that was like a fire in the sky, the clouds all ablaze and shining like they had been struck from a blacksmith's forge and the air so sweet and cool, I almost got the shivers.

Pa and Ma took to the Gonzalo family. They seemed like old friends by the time Luke and I came back to the cabin. Ma was just beaming and Pa looked as if he'd dropped ten years off his age. We were all standing on the front porch, looking at the glorious sunset when we saw a man riding up the road along the creek. He was atop a dun horse with small feet, and I knew the animal must have some Arabian blood. The man was heavily bearded, blond, with square shoulders and a square face as if he had been carved out of a block of granite. A rifle jutted from his scabbard and he was wearing a Colt revolver that was tied down to his leg.

"Ah, that is our neighbor," Gonzalo said, "Harry Blaisdell. You will like him."

"I didn't think we had any neighbors," Ma said.

"Up here, the valleys are like big fences," Gonzalo said. "And the canyons so big you could hide a city in them. He lives not far from here, but he is close only if you are a bird and can fly."

Ma laughed.

"Saw the dust when you passed by," Blaisdell said. "I'm Harry Blaisdell. Thought I'd see who you were and say hello."

Gonzalo made the introductions. Harry tied his horse to the hitchrail and joined us on the porch.

"Welcome to Lost Creek," he said.

"Is that the name of this creek?" Pa asked.

"I think they call it that because it changes course all the time. Depending on the snows and runoff. Isn't that right, Ruben?"

Gonzalo laughed. "You are right, Harry. The creek gets itself lost all the time."

Blaisdell said he had come West from St. Louis after the war and he had fought for the South, serving as a major in an artillery regiment. He looked military, with his straight, stiff back and authoritative bearing. I liked him almost immediately. He smoked a pipe and the tobacco had an enjoyable aroma to it.

"Selva tell you about the Utes?" Blaisdell asked.

"He said they probably would not give us any trouble," Pa said.

"Might be a good idea to leave some trinkets and tobacco up there near their sacred mountain. You'll find the place. Whenever they come by, they check there to see if any honor is being paid to them."

"What is their sacred mountain, exactly?" Pa asked.

"Well, it's kind of like a little shrine. The Utes have been using it for many years, maybe centuries. It's a little place next to the base of the mountain where they have left skulls of bighorn sheep and obsidian arrowheads, beads and pouches. You can't miss it, if you walk up to what we call Ute Mountain. Might help you make friends of what could be potential enemies."

"We left Texas because of the Comanches," Ma said. "They murdered our neighbors in horrible ways. They stole and burned and slaughtered. I hope the Utes are more friendly."

"They have been for some time, but, after all, this is their native country, and we're interlopers. Trespassers. After that Custer thing up in the Dakotas, Indians all over the West just might want to rise up and take back what rightfully belongs to them."

These were sobering thoughts that Blaisdell gave to us, and I wondered what awaited us when we journeyed to the high country. I was already drunk on the scent of pines and spruce and the beauty that lay around us. It would be a pity if some marauding Utes or Arapahos, which Blaisdell also spoke of, came after all of us like the Comanches had and decided to kill us.

Although Gonzalo invited Blaisdell to stay for supper, he said he had to get back home or his wife would scalp him. Everybody laughed at that, and just as it began to grow dark, our new neighbor left. I was hoping we'd see more of him after we came back down in the fall, and vowed to ask Gonzalo how to ride over to his place when we did come into winter quarters.

We all slept in the bunkhouse that night, a luxury after so many nights on hard ground. I heard the timber wolves calling through the darkness and their songs lulled me to sleep. For once, Ma and Pa didn't argue about anything, and I was sure we were entering a new phase in our lives, one where we could all enjoy a modicum of peace and contentment.

The next morning, after a good breakfast of eggs and beefsteaks, biscuits laden with butter and honey, and fresh cool milk, we gathered the herd and started out for our new home in the high country. It was a bright and sunny day, chilly at first, but warming as we rode the eighteen miles up a sometimes precarious trail.

Gonzalo explained that Selva had raised sheep here once, before the Utes assassinated his family, and some of the trails were very narrow. The trail followed the creek, and we traversed wide moraines that were ancient, with rocks and boulders strewn everywhere. The creek was lined with stands of quaking aspen that glistened green in the sun, and always, the pines towering above the land, so stately and graceful and aromatic.

When we reached the big valley several hours later, it stretched out before us like a garden in Eden. It was truly beautiful and my mother gasped at the sight. Pa's mouth dropped and his eyes widened when he saw all the lush grass and the mountains rising up on either side. We turned the cattle into the grasslands and continued on to the place where Gonzalo said we could build our new home of logs that were already cut and cured.

The place was on a plateau above the valley, with lots of trees surrounding the open space.

"And there," Gonzalo said, pointing to a huge granite mountain far off through the trees, "is Ute Mountain, a very sacred place to them."

We saw some elk moving along a nearby slope. We watched them disappear down into a ravine just above the valley. I had never seen elk before and I was amazed at their size and graceful movements through the woods.

I looked off to the south, high above the valley. There was a long ridge that seemed to be made of limestone, and at one place, a large square opening.

"What's that, Ruben?" I asked, pointing.

"Ah, *La Ventana*. The Window."

"It looks like a window, at that."

"Beyond is sacred Ute land. Do not go through the window. The Utes will not like it if you do. Even the window is sacred to them. Or magic."

"Magic?"

"The Utes believe in magic, I think. Spirits, too. Selva rode through that window, and maybe that is why his family was murdered by the Utes."

"I'll keep that in mind, Ruben."

"You do not need to go there anyway. Selva says it is a bad place."

"Why?"

"I do not know. Now, I must get back home. I will come back in two weeks and bring supplies. Your father gave me money."

Pa and Ma had signed papers the night before and I knew they had given Ruben some money on the land to show good faith, "bona fides" as Ma put it. So, now we figured we owned all this land, stretching from Ute Mountain to La Ventana.

I looked to the west, saw more mountains. The land there rose gently to a high ridge.

"How far that way does our land go?" I asked Gonzalo.

"To the ridge you see. Beyond is another very big valley with a stream running through it. Nobody owns it. It is too far, I think. But you can go there and hunt the elk and the mule deer. It is a very beautiful place and there is good hunting there."

"Thanks, Ruben. I will go there if I can."

Gonzalo left to ride the eighteen miles back down to the ranch below and his cabin. We made lean-tos out of tarps and I cut wood for a fire, while Ma made preparations for supper. Luke and Pa rode down to check on the herd. When they returned, the fire was blazing and Ma was cooking our meal. We were all hungry. The thin air gave us all appetites.

"Well, we're here," Ma said.

"Tomorrow, we'll start building our cabin," Pa said.

"The herd may be all right," Luke said. "Less'n wolves or mountain cats get at them."

"Maybe we ought to ride herd tonight," I said.

"No," Pa said. "We will see what we see in the morning. Let's have faith that all will be well."

Luke didn't say anything, but I saw a look cross his face. I don't think he believed in faith.

I didn't know if I did or not.

10

I STAYED UP LATE ON THAT PROMONTORY OVERLOOKING THE long green valley. I was looking up at the stars, but I was puzzling over some questions in my mind that had cropped up from reading the books my ma had given to me over the years. I wondered, as I sat there all alone, what I was to do in life, and some of my puzzlement came from thinking about Nora and how short her life had been. How long would I live? No one could say.

But, beyond that, I was thinking about fate and destiny. Were they both the same thing? Different sides of the same coin? Heraclitus had written that character is fate. If one is born with a certain character, does that mean the person is doomed to live with the results of that character? Euripides said that fate was the strongest thing he had ever known, giving me the impression that it was useless to try and buck one's fate.

Unless bucking fate added to one's character.

Was fate something etched in stone?

Then what about destiny? Shakespeare wrote that "it is not in the stars to hold our destiny but in ourselves." I took that to mean that we can control our destiny, but not our fate.

So, what was my fate? What was my destiny? Could I do anything about either one?

It seemed to me that night, as I gazed upward at the wise old stars that fate was something that happened to you on your way to fulfilling your destiny. But that didn't help me untangle myself from my dilemma. Was I fated to run all my life and hide from savages, be they Indians or white men? Or could I somehow find the courage to face up to the evils of the world and change my fate? And what was my destiny, then?

It seemed to me that nobody had the answer to these questions. As I sat there, my thoughts got all tangled up and I began to think that destiny and fate were probably the same thing under different names. My mind told me that destiny was something you couldn't change, that it signified what a man was to do in his life, what he was born to do. If this were so, then, what about fate? Would it cancel destiny? Or could destiny overcome fate?

I heard a wolf howl on a far ridge and the sound echoed in my mind like the questions I had been asking myself. I thought about that wolf and wondered if his fate was to die of old age, or from a Ute arrow, or a white man's bullet. Or was his destiny to be a great hunter and sire many pups so that his line could be continued?

Who was I? I asked myself. And who was I to be?

And it all came back to my biggest question. What is courage?

"Chip. It's so late."

I turned and saw the shadowy figure of my mother walking toward me.

"It's beautiful out here, Ma."

"Yes. And lonely."

She sat beside me and we both looked up at the stars. The Milky Way seemed so close, the clearest I had ever seen it. Like a river—no, an ocean—of stars, stretching across the heavens. Looking at it gave me a feeling of smallness, and loneliness, too.

"Are you lonely, Ma?"

She sighed. "Maybe just a little homesick, Chip. Are you? You must miss Nora terribly."

"I think about her every day. She would have loved it up here. I miss old Mose, too. He was a good old dog."

"You have lost a lot, Chip. You must feel very uprooted, as I do."

"Yes, but I think I'm filling up on this country, the beauty of it."

"You must always look for the beauty, my son."

"You taught me that, Ma. And I do, I guess."

We could hear the cattle, see their dark shapes in the valley below, their bodies lit by moon and starlight.

"I'm sure I'll get used to this place. Once we have a home built. It won't be the same, though. There was something harsh about Texas, but beautiful, too. The canyon. The trees, the wildlife. Even the emptiness at times."

I knew what she meant. Our ranch in Texas had been a struggle, even without the threat and depredations of the Comanches. There were times when I saw that my mother was worn out from the work and she aged before my eyes over the years. Yet, I knew she was happy inside. She had made her home there, along with my father, and she was proud of their accomplishments.

"It's so different here," I said. "All these trees and the mountains rising up everywhere you look, and the canyons, the valleys, the creeks. It all seems so rich and lush. Yet, being here makes me feel so small, so insignificant."

She patted me on the arm.

"You will grow into it, Chip. You are only as small as you think you are. The mountains will make you grow tall inside."

"Ma, you always make me feel good inside. You are the wisest person I know."

She laughed. Self-consciously, I thought. But I loved her laugh. It made me feel warm. And loved. I wondered at her ability to be cheerful at times when Pa and I were morose and downhearted. She could laugh and raise our spirits. That, I thought, was a rare gift.

"Do not tarry long here," she said. "I'm very tired and now I can sleep. Knowing you are all right."

"Yes. I was just out here, thinking about things."

"Good thoughts, I hope."

"Yes."

I wanted to talk to her about courage and fate and destiny, but I knew she was tired and there was a lot on her mind.

"Good night, Chip," she said.

"Good night, Ma."

She got up and I watched her walk back to the lean-to. The dark swallowed her up and I was again alone on the edge of the world. It was turning very cold and I wondered if the cattle would keep their summer coats up this high or grow winter hair for these chilly nights. I began to shiver and my eyes became droopy. My mind emptied and I got up and walked back to our camp, listening to my soft footsteps, so crisp and defined in that rarified mountain air.

I fell asleep looking at the ground outside the lean-to that was bathed in starlight. Pa was snoring and I could hear my mother breathing. She was fast asleep. Luke was stretched out nearby, out in the open, flat on his back, his rifle next to him.

I dreamed of wolves and elk with long sweeping horns

like some of our cattle, and there was a dark girl jumping over a small stream that threaded through a long green valley, and I chased after her only to see her change into a dog much like Mose, and he stood on his hind legs and danced until his coat turned the color of blood and he evaporated in a stand of trees with their leaves turning russet and I was suddenly cold as if the moonlight was a frost that coated my dream body in soft silver that dripped from me like water and left small puddles where I walked in that desolate dreamscape, where wolves perched in trees and called like sleepy owls across the dark, while the wind whimpered in my ears like a lost girl calling out my name from a place beyond all reason and in a language understood only by dreamers.

11

I BOILED UP OUT OF MY BEDROLL JUST AFTER DAWN, MY mother's screams ripping through the still air. I grabbed my rifle without thinking and dashed out from under the lean-to. Pa was right behind me. Ma stood near the stack of logs, frozen in fear, her eyes wide, her face drawn and blanched.

Then I heard it, and looked down at the ground.

There in front of the pile of logs was a big timber rattler, coiled up, its beaded tail buzzing at a frantic rate.

"Don't move, Ma," I said, walking up to the left, cocking my Winchester.

She held her breath and stared at the snake as if hypnotized.

The rattler's head moved and I knew it was looking at me now. I stopped, raised the rifle to my shoulder and drew a bead on his head. I lined up the front blade sight with the rear buckhorn, held my breath and slowly squeezed the trigger. The rifle bucked against my shoulder as flame and smoke spewed from the muzzle. I heard the bullet hit something solid. The snake began to wriggle and thrash and my mother screamed again.

I walked up, jacking another cartridge into the chamber of my rifle, prepared to shoot again in case I had missed.

Luke emerged out of the trees and walked around behind me, where Pa had come to watch. Both of them carried rifles, but neither looked ready to shoot.

"What the hell . . ." Luke said.

"I think you got him, Chip," Pa said. He pointed to a place near the lowest log, and there was a dark lump there.

The snake continued to wriggle, but it wasn't going anywhere in particular. I looked at the thrashing snake and saw that its head was gone. There was just a pinkish blob of flesh where its deadly fangs had been.

"It's all right, Ma," I said, stepping over to her. I grabbed her with one arm. She was trembling as if gripped with the ague.

"Lordy, he scared me," she gasped.

"He's dead, Ma."

"Why-why is it still twisting all around?"

"Its head is gone. It can't bite."

"Stay away from that woodpile, Mercy," Luke said. "I think the rattler was more scared of you than you were of it."

Ma laughed, releasing the pent-up energy that had built up in her through fear. She relaxed in the cradle of my arm and I stepped away.

"Close call," Pa said, examining the snake, which continued to writhe, although much of its energy was draining away. I looked at its head and its mouth was moving too. I could see the fangs showing and the sight sent a chill up my spine.

Then the fear of what might have happened hit me and I started to tremble. Then I began shaking all over. My mother didn't notice. She was still rattled from the experience. But

Luke came over and looked me straight in the eye, a faint curl of a smile on his lips.

"Buck fever, huh? Or maybe snake fever."

"I-I don't know, Luke. I-I can't stop shaking."

"That happens. You done real good, Chip."

Ma looked at me.

"Chip, what's the matter?" she asked.

I shook my head. I didn't know. "That snake's head, moving like that, just put the fear in me."

"He'll be all right," Luke said. "He's got the shakes from being so close to that snake."

"But he killed it," Ma said. "He probably saved my life."

"He did that without thinking, Mercy," Luke said. "Now, he's thinking about what a close call it was."

I nodded, all numb inside.

Pa came over and looked at me. He shook his head and the expression on his face was one of disgust.

"Chip always was a scaredy-cat," Pa said. "Least sign of danger when he was a kid and he'd run and hide."

"Keith, stop it," Ma said. She put a hand on my arm.

"Well, it's so," Pa said. "No gettin' around it. Chip, deep down, is a bona-fide coward, ain't you, Chip?"

I nodded, but I was trying to get over the shakes more than trying to agree with my father. I couldn't look at that snake head and I wanted to get as far away from it as I could. I looked at my mother, a silent pleading in my eyes.

"Come on and sit down, Chip, under the lean-to. I'll fix breakfast. You'll be all right."

"Yes'm."

She walked me back to the lean-to and sat me down. I huddled up and held my shaking hands out in front of me, then clamped them together to try and stop them from trembling. I hung my head, ashamed of myself.

"You're not a coward, Chip. Your father . . . he . . . he . . . well, sometimes . . ."

I waited for her to finish her sentence, but she choked up and turned away. She began rummaging through one of the boxes where our food was stored. I walked outside. Pa and Luke were starting the cookfire in a place that had been used before, a blackened circle ringed by stones that were also blackened by previous fires.

The horses were skittery and I went off to see what was making them jumpy. They had all been hobbled for the night and were nickering to be let loose. To mollify them, I gave them grain, oats, and corn, then started walking around, looking for a corral. My stomach was still upset from the turmoil and food was the last thing I wanted just then. Way back in the trees, well away from camp, I found the remains of one old corral, and another that had been burned some time ago. One could be repaired, and the outlines of the other were still visible. I could build a corral there, and I found another place that would give me still another, should the ranch grow and we had need for more horses.

I heard Ma calling me to breakfast, but I kept walking away from our camp until I no longer heard the clanking of pans and the scrape of forks on pewter plates. I looked for snakes everywhere I walked. I sat on a deadfall and listened to the sounds of morning, the birds, the insects, the whispering songs of the breezes in the trees. I guess I was feeling sorry for myself and knew I had to get over it right quick.

Luke and Pa had set the foundation logs by the time I got back to our camp. Ma gave me hot coffee and I pitched in, grabbing an axe and chipping notches in the logs that Pa had marked for me. We worked right up until noon, when the sun was at its zenith, straight overhead. Pa and I didn't speak much, and Luke kept his counsel. Ma busied herself organizing our goods and planning things in her mind. Every so often, I could hear her humming to herself and I knew she was happy, or trying to be.

In a few days, we had the main walls of the cabin up, windows and gun ports cut, and in another two days, we had the roof on. We all helped with the chinking. Luke built a stone sled and we hauled rocks in for the fireplace, which Pa built in the front room. Ma made herself a kitchen and wrote down things she would need to buy when we left for the winter. The main item she had was a wood stove for her kitchen, which we built on out back. The place was beginning to look like a home and there was room for all of us inside the log house.

"I'm going to ride up to Ute Mountain today," Pa announced one morning. "Anybody want to go with me? I'm going to look for that shrine that Gonzalo told us about, put out some things for the Utes, case they come by."

"We'll all go," Ma said. "I think we need an outing. You boys have all worked hard and I'm ready for a change of scenery. I'll pack us a basket lunch."

Luke and I saddled the horses. It was the first chance I'd had to talk to him alone.

"You shouldn't pay your pa no mind about what he said when you got the williwaws over that rattler, Chip."

"I've always been afraid of snakes."

"Lots of folks are scared of snakes and spiders and such."

"I mean really terrified, Luke. Because of what happened."

"With your ma?"

"No, something that happened when I was a kid. To my pa and me."

"You got scared by a snake? You and your pa?"

I took in a breath and let it out quick. I hadn't talked to anyone about this in all my life and had tried to put it out of my mind. But, that morning, when Ma had that rattler after her, it all came back.

"Did you know I had a little brother, Luke?"

He shook his head.

"His name was James, but we called him Digger, because he was always digging in the dirt for worms and bugs and we thought it was pretty funny. I guess he was about six when this happened, and I was eight years old. James was digging out by the woodpile and our pa was splitting logs into kindling wood. I was sharpening one of the axes. James screamed and there was a sidewinder coiled up right in front of a hole he had dug. There were eggs, snake eggs, in the hole, I reckon."

"More likely turtle eggs," Luke said.

"Pa had his rifle leaning against the rick of wood he had just cut and he had a pistol strapped on, too. James screamed and the snake buzzed and got ready to strike. I told Pa to shoot the snake, but he started shaking like I was shaking this morning and he just stood there. That scared me, too, and I lost my voice. Then I really got scared. The snake struck James in the face. James fell back and tried to fight it off. The snake kept coiling and uncoiling and striking James in the face and neck and my pa just stood there. And then he ran. He ran like a damned coward. James started whimpering and then he got real still and his face turned blue."

"Jesus," Luke said.

"The snake turned on me, then, and I ran like I was on fire. I ran to the house and Pa was inside, just blubbering to himself while Ma tried to make sense of it. She saw me and asked me what was going on and I just said 'James. Snake.' Ma snatched the pistol out of Pa's holster and ran out to the woodpile. I heard a shot, then a couple more. I was sitting on the floor of the kitchen shivering like a dog shitting peach seeds.

"Ma came back carrying little James in her arms. He wasn't breathing and I knew he was dead."

"No wonder," Luke said.

"I ran like a sissy, Luke, when I could have saved my little brother."

"What did your pa say?"

"He asked Ma if she had killed the snake, and she just looked at him, slammed his pistol down on the table, and walked into the bedroom with James. Pa never mentioned it after that, and neither did Ma or I. It was just forgotten. Until this morning."

"Your pa didn't run today," Luke said.

"No, but he didn't do anything, either. And I shot the snake before I even thought about it. I thought maybe I wasn't afraid anymore, but when I saw that snake's head, it reminded me of that one sidewinder biting James to death and I got real scared all over again."

"You had good reason."

"Have you ever been that scared, Luke? So scared you turned coward?"

"No man wants to admit to cowardice, Chip. And I don't really know what it is. I've been scared, sure. And I've wanted to run like hell from danger. But you can't label a man a coward for one moment of fear."

"Then when do you label someone a coward?"

"Boy, you ask really knotty questions, Chip. I guess I probably know more about not being a coward than the other way around."

"What do you mean?"

"Maybe we're all cowards at heart. Deep down. But, it's how a man deals with cowardice that makes up his measure."

"I don't know if I understand what you mean."

"You can run away from something, I think. But if you run back, then you're not a coward."

"In other words, you face up to your fear and try to conquer it."

"You put it in words better'n me. Yeah, I guess that's what I mean. A man can be a coward for one minute, or one second, and it don't count too much. But if he always runs from trouble or danger, then I reckon you could brand him a coward. There's mice and there's lions in this world."

"But can a mouse become a lion?"

"Chip, I don't know. I just don't know."

I shook my head.

I didn't know either.

12

UTE MOUNTAIN.

It rose up from a flat plain of hard pan like an ancient fortress. From its height and position, I could see that it afforded a commanding view of the land in all directions to anyone standing atop it. When I looked up at it, I almost expected to see a Ute warrior standing there looking down on us.

However, there were no signs of life anywhere around it. It was eerily quiet, with only a whisper of a breeze blowing across the flat plain where the four of us had ridden. The mountain stood stark against the surrounding, tree-studded mountains, bare, gaunt, forbidding, and oddly majestic, as if it had been created as a landmark, a treeless monument in the midst of a thousand forests.

"I wonder where that shrine thing is," Pa said, gazing around as if bewildered. It was a rhetorical question and no one answered him. Because no one knew. Luke dismounted and stooped over, examining the flat, pebble-strewn plateau on which we found ourselves. He picked up an object and turned it over in his hand. I dismounted and pulled my horse over to him.

"What have you got, Luke?"

"An arrowhead. Like none I've ever seen before."

The arrowhead shone black in the sun, its chipped sides glinting like shined leather, very shiny. I touched it. The edges were razor sharp. Someone had taken care to fashion it; the notches were deep, but the bottom part was thick so that it would not break easily.

"It's obsidian," I said.

"Not flint?"

"No, Luke. It's a different mineral. Very fancy, compared to flint."

We both looked around. The ground was littered with shards of obsidian arrowheads, most of them broken, as if flawed and cast away by the artisans. We saw traces of old campfires as we walked around, leading our horses, while Ma and Pa rode up to the face of the mountain. Luke and I walked to the edge of the plateau and heard something down below.

"Well, I'll be damned," he said.

"What?"

"There's a running stream down there. You can barely hear it."

The ground showed signs of wear, with several paths leading down to the creek, which I could hear burbling faintly when I listened closely.

"I wonder why they didn't camp down there, hidden in the trees?" I asked.

"Dunno. If they carried water up here, it don't seem natural. A lot of work."

"Maybe they wanted to camp away from the creek because of the noise," I said. "Maybe they wanted to be able to hear if anyone rode up on them."

"Could be."

We found lots of places where the Utes had made cook-fires and at one end of the plateau, below in the trees, there were heaps of human offal, long since desiccated and without aroma. There were lots of animal bones scattered around, deer, elk, smaller animals, birds.

"They must have summered here, Luke."

"A good spot. They could put a lookout up on that mountain and he could holler down here to their camp. Give them plenty of time to run off or get ready to defend themselves."

"Luke, Chip," Pa hollered. "Come on over here."

We looked around, saw Ma and Pa way down at the prow of the mountain. They were both waving at us to ride over.

"There it is," Pa said, pointing to a niche in the rock. A large niche that appeared to have been hollowed out, over time, by water running fast and hard around that part of the mountain. There was what looked like a small grotto. About three feet off the ground, maybe four, there was a rocky ledge above the watermark. The ground was smooth around it, with indications that water had flowed past it, wiping the ground free of large rocks and most pebbles.

Strewn around on the ledge of the "shrine" were eerie objects that made our skin crawl. These were down inside the hollow of the small cavern, keeping them free of the spring run-off. There was a pair of very tiny moccasins, beaded with strange symbols in different colors, red, yellow, green, blue, black, and white. And there was an arrow jutting from the crown with feathers that looked as if they might have come from an eagle's wing. There was the skull of a Rocky Mountain bighorn sheep, with massive horns, deep eye-socket holes, a single black hole in the center of the skull. There were various trinkets: a bracelet of beads; a breast-plate made from the bones of a large bird or a small animal, sewn together with sinew; a gold locket that appeared to have once belonged to a white woman; a broken knife with a blade of chipped obsidian; a worn-out leather quiver with a single arrow in it; some empty clay bowls; and various small bones from rabbits or other small animals.

"Well, I'll be damned," Luke breathed.

"Look at that odd board with leather straps," Ma said. "Leaning against the rock there."

"What is it?" I asked.

"I think it's what they carry their babies in," Ma said. "If you look close, you'll see a tiny skeleton inside those straps. It appears to be very old."

I saw it then, and chill bumps crept up my arm. The hackles on the back of my neck stood up, quivered like tuning forks.

"This is their shrine," I whispered. "We'd better get the hell out of here."

We all looked around to see if anyone was watching. The wind whistled around the edge of the mountain and gave us all a sudden chill. It was so quiet at that moment, we could hear each of us breathing.

"I'm going to leave some things here," Pa said, "to show the Utes we mean them no harm."

"What kind of things?" Ma asked.

"I don't know. Something they can use, or that will show them we have respect."

"This is a kind of sacred grave, too, I think," Ma said.

"You mean because of the baby's skeleton," I said.

"Not only that. But a kind of grave marking past events in the lives of these people. Mementos of important things, maybe."

"Then maybe we ought to be careful what we put on that ledge, Pa."

"I'll have to give that some thought," Pa said. "Let's get out of here. This place gives me the williwaws."

"It's sure as hell spooky," Luke said, and that surprised me. Luke has always seemed unaffected by strange or odd things, either dismissing them without much comment, or reflecting on them rather dispassionately. But there was mystery here in this place, and whispers of unimaginable rituals or ceremonies that were beyond our understanding. There was the feeling that we had walked into a place which an ancient people held dear and sacred. It felt as if we had walked into a graveyard guarded by unseen spirits. There was a chill in the air that seemed to have come up with a startling suddenness, as if we were intruders and were being warned by those invisible spirits.

"Yeah," I said. "Let's get out of here."

We turned our horses back toward our camp, and then all stopped as we glimpsed something in the sky, something that should not have been there.

"Looky yonder," Luke said, his voice low and husky as if he had something lodged in his throat. He pointed to a tree-studded ridge directly opposite Ute Mountain.

A puff of smoke, round as a ball, rose in the air, white and stark against the clear blue bowl of the sky.

Then another, rising slowly. Then three quick small puffs. As the smoke climbed, the air currents blew them apart and they shredded into wisps, then vanished.

"What in hell is that?" Pa asked, his voice barely above a whisper.

"It's smoke," Ma said.

"Somebody's makin' it," Luke said.

Then two more quick puffs and then another single one, larger than the others.

"Some kind of message," I muttered.

"A damned Ute message, if you ask me," Luke said.

"Luke," Ma said, "don't talk like that. You scare me."

We waited and watched, but there was no more smoke from that place. I scanned the horizon all around, looking for . . . what, I did not know. But maybe an answer from another place.

Pa turned and looked behind us. I saw his face turn rigid and the color drain from it.

"My God," he said. "There's some more back there."

We all turned around, and, sure enough, we saw more puffs of smoke, a long way from Ute Mountain, but plainly visible. A whole series of puffs hung motionless above a far peak, plainly visible for miles around.

"An answer," I said.

"I wish I knew what they're saying," Ma said.

But I think we all knew what the smoke signals were saying. Luke was the one who expressed what was in our thoughts.

"The Utes know we're here," he said.

"What will they do?" Ma asked.

Luke shook his head.

"Damned if I know. But we'd better keep a lookout. One of these days, we just might have some unwelcome visitors."

The smoke signals disappeared and it seemed, for a moment, that they had never happened, that, perhaps, we had imagined those little puffs of smoke in the sky.

But on the ride back down to camp, I knew this was not true.

We had seen the smoke, and we all were aware that the Utes knew we were there and that we had been to their sacred mountain.

I just hoped they were not mad that we had come here and would leave us alone.

But in my heart I knew that those smoke signals meant that we were all in danger.

The Utes had not gone away. They were still here.

And we were trespassing on sacred ground.

13

ONCE THE CABIN WAS FINISHED, LUKE KILLED A TWO-YEAR-old cow and Pa butchered it, so we'd have fresh meat.

"We can't keep eatin' our herd, Chip," Pa said. "So, maybe you better do some huntin'. We could use one of them muley deer or a small elk, I reckon."

I had been itching to hunt anyway, so Pa's request was most welcome. I had helped him take some things up to the Ute shrine and leave them, the day before. He and I had ridden up to Ute Mountain carrying one of Ma's felt hats, an apron she had made, some calico cloth, part of a bolt left over from Ma's sewing, and a box of sequins and beads. Ma also put some pins and needles in a little red pincushion that looked like a tomato, along with some colored thread, all inside a little wicker basket with a top on it that fastened shut with a looped thong.

"You put food out for 'em," Pa said, "and the critters'll eat it, so we won't do none of that."

"You reckon the Utes will know we mean them no harm, Pa?"

"We'll check back every now and then and see if any of these things are gone. At least we'll know they come here and look for offerings."

Pa and I rode back down to our new cabin feeling pretty good about the things we had left for the Utes. We had seen no more smoke signals and thought maybe they knew we were just up there ranching, not hostile or anything.

I took my rifle and pistol, some ammunition, a canteen and something to eat, jerky, hardtack, and some dried apples and rode up a narrow trail over the ridge behind us, which looked most promising for finding wild game up in that high wilderness. I rode my cow pony, Dan, a three-year-old gelding. Dan was surefooted and gentle, and I could shoot from the saddle on him without him running out from under me. Dan was my hunting horse, not only for game, but for stray cattle back in Texas. He seemed used to the high altitude, as was I, and I wouldn't run him hard anyway. He seemed eager to get away from the other horses and explore some new country.

Dan and I reached the top of the ridge and looked out on a vast expanse of mountains and valleys. Evergreens rose up in thick tiers on every slope, and beyond, snowcapped peaks shone a brilliant white in the sun. It was truly a breathtaking view and the sheep or game trail I was on branched out into many trails, all streaming from that point in various directions. To my left and over my shoulder, I could see La Ventana, that mysterious window through the rim rock of that long ridge, and I wondered what lay beyond. But I knew that place, too, was sacred to the Utes, so I turned my gaze on the vast valley below and through the trees, I saw the glint of a stream shining silver in the sun.

I stayed on the main trail and headed for the valley far below. The trail switched back and forth so that some of the steepness was taken out of the ride. Soon, Dan and I were in thick pines, interspersed with fir, spruce, and juniper.

There was one large juniper that appeared as if it had been hit by a bomb and exploded. Upon closer examination, I saw the tine marks and figured this had been done by a huge bull elk during the rut, marking its territory. I was amazed at the damage a set of antlers could do to a juniper. It appeared to have been blasted with cannonballs.

There was a path, which appeared to be another sheep trail, branching off to the right. There was something odd about it, though, and when I rode down it I was surprised to see moccasin tracks that looked very fresh. When I back-tracked, I realized what had caught my eye. There were no footprints on the trail I had been riding, but upon closer examination I saw that there probably had been, and not long before I rode down it. There were marks in the soft earth showing that someone had swept the tracks clean, probably with a pine or fir branch. The small lines were unmistakably made by something resembling a broom. Except the lines left by the sweeper were curved and erratic such as might have been left by a pine branch with clusters of needles just like broom straw.

Why, I wondered, would someone try to conceal their tracks, way up here in the Rockies? I was on my guard as I continued following the trail, which was wiped so smooth, it was like a track, even with no tracks. I pulled my rifle from its scabbard and lay it across my lap, ready to lever a cartridge into the chamber. My Colt single-action pistol was within easy reach.

I was riding down a blind trail so I kept some of my attention on Dan. He was just sensitive enough and new enough to this country to give me fair warning if there was anything out of ordinary up ahead, like a bear or a mountain lion. But I knew that no animal had brushed away those tracks and I was both curious and cautious. Perhaps too curious, I thought.

I kept track of my bearings, and every so often I caught

a glimpse of Ute Mountain off to my right, higher up. Below, the mountain dropped off steeply, but there were plenty of trees between me and the bottom, so I wasn't worried about falling off some of the more narrow passages. I wondered if I was following a sheep trail or a game trail, and decided, after a while, that it was the latter. No one in their right mind would drive sheep through thick forest on such a narrow trail, unless there was some kind of magical grass at the end. The trail was well-worn, at that, but I saw no animal tracks. There were signs of a recent rain and perhaps the runoff had wiped away all signs. I continued to see signs that whoever had come this way before me was still dragging a big pine branch behind him.

Then I saw part of an unshod pony track where the pine needles had skipped over a piece of earth. That was not very encouraging, but I kept on, fascinated by the country, country that seemed to open up to me each hundred yards or so. Below, where the trees grew, I saw a lot of downed pine trees, and I saw three elk move off their beds and slink through the woods, heading away from me on a parallel course. I wondered how such large animals could move so silently, never breaking a twig or a dry branch, never jostling a tree limb.

The trail began to rise slightly and above me I saw rim rock, as if a small ridge had threaded through the trees in a more or less straight line. Then the path dipped some and began to fade out for a time. I began to see outcroppings of rock that looked like ancient ruins, all mossy and overgrown, silent, brooding, eerie in the silence.

Dan was showing no signs that there was any danger ahead, but still showed curiosity at the rocky outcroppings, the deadfalls, and the strong scent of bear scat at one place where the rocks gaped with black cave holes. Dan snorted and seemed ready to bolt, but I kept him on a tight rein.

Now there were trails leading off from the one I was on, which was not unusual. I came across a blazed tree, though, which was. I stopped to look at the scar on the pine tree a short foot off the trail I was on. It was old, and not horse high. That meant, to me, that someone had walked this way some time in the past with a hatchet and marked this trail. Why? What were they after? What did they expect to find? From that point, I had a clear view of the back end of Ute Mountain, but that didn't help illuminate the mystery. I sighed and rode on, looking for more blazed trees and pony tracks.

The game trail began to lead to a higher elevation and when I topped a thickly wooded rise, I saw a most beautiful sight. There, just ahead of me, was a wide long meadow, perhaps ten or twelve acres in size, and, too, a clear look at Ute Mountain. Above the meadow, there was a graceful waterfall, with a long straight drop of perhaps fifty feet or so. The waterfall generated a clear stream that ran through the meadow, a meadow burning green in the sunlight with lush grasses and blooming Columbine and other flowers I could not name.

I waited there for a long moment, drinking in the absolute beauty of that place, and now I thought I knew why there was at least one blaze along that trail. Someone, long ago, might have discovered this place and wanted to return to it. So, perhaps, the tree had been blazed with a hatchet on the walk back. But why not just hike up to Ute Mountain and complete the circle? Another mystery, and I was thoroughly baffled.

I touched my heels to Dan's flanks and he entered the meadow. We rode to the edge of the stream and I reined up. Dan bent his neck and drank from the bubbling clear waters flowing past us. Above me, there was blue sky and at every surround, a magnificent vista. I saw far off snowcapped

mountain peaks and phalanxes of evergreens rising in staggered profusion above the huge valley far below.

Dan finished drinking and I turned him downstream,
thinking to ride over the edge of the meadow and journey
down into the thick woods and start tracking game. I had
already decided I would come back this way and ride up to
Ute Mountain then ride downhill to our cabin. I knew Ma
was finishing the chinking today and Pa and Luke were
building a corral where we could brand calves in the
spring.

Dan and I edged off the meadow and headed down a
steep slope into the trees. I was looking for another game
trail when Dan's ears perked up, stiffened, and began twisting in half arcs, trying to pick up some small sound. I
pulled in on the reins and we stopped. Dan listened. I listened. I saw a hawk float overhead, wings spread wide, riding the air currents. A red-tailed hawk, I thought, before it
disappeared. I heard only the burbling of the stream which
was meandering downhill in the same direction Dan and I
were headed.

I felt Dan quivering beneath me and saw the muscles in
his legs rippling under his hide. He turned his head and his
ears twisted like twin cones, the sunlight making the small
hairs lining the edges glow like filaments.

Then I heard the snick of a rifle lock, as if someone had
cocked a hammer back. My blood froze and shivers sizzled
up my spine like icy fingers stroking my back.

I ducked and snaked my rifle from the cradle of the saddle and started to cock the lever.

"Do not move," a voice said, and I heard something
scrape against a tree. Dan and I both turned at the same
time.

I saw movement, then a patch of color that looked like a
deer. But it wasn't a deer. Because right above it, the black

snout of a rifle seemed to grow right out of the tall pine tree. And the muzzle was pointed straight at me.

I knew then that I was just a short trigger pull away from death.

14

So many things go through your mind when you're faced with danger or death. But most of them fly by so fast you can't grasp them or sort them out. None of this happened to me, however. I just looked at that black hole at the end of a rifle barrel and wondered if I'd hear the explosion or just see the orange flame and smoke before everything turned dark.

My rifle turned heavy in my hand and I didn't know what to do with it. If I moved it, whoever was standing behind that tree was going to blow my head off. I let the barrel drop ever so slowly to rest on the edge of the pommel and wished I was back in Texas with Nora still alive.

I lifted my left arm, which felt stupid, but I had only one arm free to raise and I wanted the rifleman to know that I meant no harm and was surrendering, if that's what he wanted me to do.

I sat there, one arm floating above my head, feeling like an idiot, when the man stepped out from behind the tree, the rifle in his hands leveled at my head or chest. I was too rattled to know which.

He was built like a pickle barrel, all round and buck-skinned. The buckskins looked very thin and light. He wore a battered hat with a wide brim and high crown, a single eagle feather sticking out of the band, and raked to a jaunty angle. His face was as round as his body, and the color of coffee that had been laced with cream, his skin not brown, not white, but somewhere in between. He had no facial hair, and his lips were surprisingly thin, his nose small and slightly hooked, with dark brown eyes flanking it, giving his face the appearance of a hawk.

"I been watching you, white boy," he said, and there was no threat nor animosity in his voice, a voice that was grav-elly and guttural as a file being rubbed over a hollow wooden turkey call very slowly, with none of the screech-ing. His voice sounded odd to me.

I didn't know what to say, so I said nothing.

He lowered the barrel of his rifle slightly and I took that as a good sign. Maybe he wasn't going to shoot me out of the saddle after all. But I was shaking inside as if my stomach was boiling with a high fever.

"I am not going to shoot you," he said. "Put your rifle away and we will smoke."

I didn't know what he meant about smoking since I had not taken up the habit, but I sheathed my rifle.

"Get down. Tie up your horse. Come and sit."

I did as I was told and we sat under a large juniper growing on the hillside. The branches shaded us.

"I am called Bear," he said, as he brought out a pipe and pouch of tobacco from a leather sack he carried slung over a sash around his ample waist. "My father was a full-blood Ute and my mother was a white woman. I am what you call a half-breed. Or just a breed they call me sometimes."

He filled the bowl of his pipe with tobacco from the small pouch. Then he pulled out a magnifying glass, held it up to the sun at an angle so that a beam lanced into the tobacco. In moments, smoke began to curl up from the pipe bowl as Bear puffed on the pipestem. He drew smoke into his mouth and lungs, then expelled it. He handed the pipe to me.

"Smoke," he said.

"I do not yet smoke."

"You will smoke now. With me."

I wiped his spit off the pipe and stuck the stem into my mouth. I sucked in air and smoke filled my mouth and burned into my lungs. I choked and lights danced in the darkness of my head. I coughed and blew the smoke out.

Bear laughed.

"Good. You have smoked."

"I don't like it much."

Then the half-breed did something with his pipe and hands. He puffed hard, taking a lot of smoke into his mouth, so much that his cheeks bulged out like a squirrel's with a mouth full of acorns. Then he held his hand over his lips and let out a little smoke. He moved his hand and the smoke rose up. He did this several times.

"Have you seen this kind of smoke before?" he asked.

"Smoke signals?"

His face lit up with his smile. He nodded.

"Yes." He pointed back to Ute mountain and then to the peaks beyond the valley below. "From there and there."

"Yes. We saw them. Was that you?"

He shook his head. "No. But I saw them too. Do you read the smoke in the sky?"

"No. I didn't know what they meant. Utes, I suppose."

He nodded and puffed his pipe. Then he handed it to me again. I shook my head, but his look told me that I was expected to smoke it. I wiped off the stem and puffed a small amount of smoke, trying to keep it from going into my chest. But I choked anyway.

I ejected the smoke from my mouth as if it were a poison gas and handed the pipe back to Bear. He seemed satisfied that I had performed the ritual.

"Do you know of Yellow Hair?" Bear asked.

I shook my head.

"He is the Army general called Custer."

"I've heard of Custer. I think he's dead, though."

"Yes. He is dead. That is what the smoke was saying. My people, the Ute tribe, say that an Ogallala man, of the Lakota tribe, one called Crazy Horse, rubbed out this Custer and his whole army at a place called the Little Big Horn, a river in the land of the Lakota."

"I didn't know that. People in Pueblo were talking about it, I think. The story was in the newspapers."

Bear nodded.

"The Ute, they say it is time for them to drive out the white eyes. The smoke writing tells of a council. A Ute chief, who is called Umiya, calls for a war council before the Moon of the Turning Leaves, August, in English, at a place in the Valley of the Window."

"Why are you telling me all this, Bear?"

"Because I think you and your family are in great danger. Umiya does not want the white eyes or the Mexicans to live on Lost Creek or anywhere in the mountains. He does not like Ruben Gonzalo and he hates Harry Blaisdell. And, now, you have come to this place near the sacred mountain and La Ventana. Yes, it is very dangerous for you to stay here."

"You are a Ute," I said. "At least part of you is. Yet, you are warning me. Are you mad at this chief Umiya?"

Bear puffed on his pipe and his eyes grew cloudy as if the smoke had crept up inside his head and filled his sockets with tobacco fumes.

"I fear him," Bear said.

His words were chilling to me. If Bear, who was part Ute, feared this Ute chief, then perhaps we all had cause for alarm. If what he had told me was true, then we were all in danger. I felt my world crumbling, for I had come to love the mountains and the house we had made, the valley where our cattle fed and grew fat, the scent of pines and the crisp air that filled my lungs.

"Do you really think this Umiya will attack us? We are so few and we mean no harm."

Bear finished his pipe and tapped the bowl against the tree, freeing the dottle, which fell to the ground. He put his hand on the ashes to see if they were still hot and then covered them over with dirt, smoothing the earth so that there was no sign of what lay beneath. He stood up. "Come," he said. "I will take you to meet my family."

I got up and walked over to my horse. Bear walked with me.

"Umiya will go on the warpath," he said. "The Arapahos gave him the news about Yellow Hair and Crazy Horse and they say all the tribes will go against the white eyes and drive them all out of the country."

"Are the Utes friends with the Arapahos?" I asked, untying my reins and pulling Dan away from the bushes.

"Sometimes. Now, I think they may join the Utes to fight the white men and drive them all away."

"They will lose," I said, with a false bravado that I hoped did not show. "There are too many white men. There are a lot of soldiers in Pueblo and in Santa Fe and back east."

"I know. Yes, they will not drive the white eyes away. But, if not, they will want their blood to mark the land. They will want to fight until the death so that their spirits can taunt the white eyes."

"Do you believe that? That their ghosts can come back?"

"Come," he said. "We will talk as we walk to my camp.

It is not far." He put his pipe away and started walking. Dan and I followed.

"My mother taught me to read and write and when she escaped from the tribe, she took me to a white man's school. I was very confused because I knew only the Ute ways. The priests did talk about one spirit, though, and so I wondered if my people were right about this. They believe in a Great Spirit and that those who have died are still with us, as ghosts in the night. And they believe that the spirits of dead human beings can come back and go into owls and wolves and bears and elk and deer, even into the ant and the lizard and the snake. I believe this may be so, but I do not know. The priests confused me, but they taught me much."

"I can understand why."

"This is the reason we came to the sacred mountain, so I could find out what is true. Also, I came to trap so that I can feed my little family. Before we leave, in the Moon of the Flying Leaves, I will stay on the mountain and not take food until I have a vision that tells me what I must believe and know."

We crossed a small creek and entered a large meadow. Across the meadow, in one corner near some tall evergreen trees, I saw a tent. There was a horse and two small burros grazing nearby. Smoke rose in the air from a campfire near the tent and I saw a small boy running around with a stick, chasing after some kind of ball.

"That is Turtle," Bear said. "My son."

We soon were at Bear's campsite and his wife, who had been inside the tent, came out. She was dressed in a white elkskin dress, her black hair trailing down her back in a single braid. She looked to be fullblood Ute, or Indian, anyway, and she was very beautiful.

"This is my wife Willow. She speaks English, and so does my son. I taught them because we must live in both worlds, that of the Ute and that of the white man."

"I thought maybe you were an outcast from the tribe," I said, and wished that I had bit my tongue.

Bear laughed.

"That is true. I am an outcast from my own house, but I am still considered a Ute by my people."

"He is more Ute than many who say they are," Willow said and I liked her immediately. "Come and sit. Will you smoke? Will you have some whiskey to drink?"

I waved my hands.

Bear laughed.

"He does not smoke," he said. "I do not know if he drinks."

"I have tasted strong drink, but I don't like it much," I said. "Thank you anyway. I am not thirsty."

"Do you speak the Spanish?" Willow asked, and I shook my head.

"Only a few words I learned down in Texas."

"I forgot," Bear said. "We all speak Spanish, too."

I was amazed at these people. I saw that they were perfectly at home in the mountains and I was sure they did all right in civilization, too. They were resourceful.

I sat down well away from the fire on a log that served as a primitive divan. Turtle came up, finally, pushing the ball, which I saw was made out of hides, with his stick. He seemed very shy, but he shook my hand at his mother's insistence and he sat down, too. One of the burros brayed and the boy got up and walked over to it and petted it, lovingly, I thought.

"That is his pet burro," Willow said. "He would sleep with it if I would let him."

"We want to be friends with you," Bear said, and I thought his tone was solemn. "We have watched you for many days and you seem to be a man who means no harm to the earth."

"No, I reckon I don't."

"You must be careful. Watch for the talking smoke in

the sky. Do not go through La Ventana and do not climb the sacred mountain. Perhaps Umiya will not harm you."

"Why do you think he will go on the warpath?" I asked. "Because of the talking smoke?"

Willow gave her husband a look and he gave her one back.

"He told me what he was going to do many moons ago," Bear said. "I know he will do this, and the smoke talk tells me this is so."

"How is it that you are an outcast from the tribe, but Umiya still told you these things?" I asked.

Bear looked at me, and there was that cloudiness in his eyes once again. He seemed to look right through me and into me and his gaze was so piercing I instinctively flinched inside.

Willow froze where she stood and little Turtle let out a long sigh and grew silent as dew on a leaf.

"Umiya is my father," he said.

15

CHIEF UMIYA OF THE UTES MUST HAVE BEEN A CRUEL MAN, I thought, after learning that he was Bear's father. I could see that it pained Bear to admit that it was his own father who had banished him from the tribe. I still didn't know why his father had treated him so badly, but my raised eyebrows were a question waiting for an answer.

"My mother ran away from my father," Bear said, as if reading my mind. "She took me to her people and this was a raw wound in my father's heart. He did not understand that my mother longed to be with her own kind. He said that she was ungrateful and that he had given her a home and a good life with his own people, a better life than she could ever have with the white eyes."

"I am sorry," I said.

"It is of no matter. We each have a path to follow in this life, and I am on mine, my father is on his. It may be that our paths will cross again one day."

I wanted to ask him about Willow, but I did not want to do it while she was there. I mulled over what Bear had told me and realized that I would probably never understand his life or the ways of the Ute. It was no wonder that Umiya wanted to make war with the whites. He thought our ways were wrong and we thought his ways were wrong.

"You are hunting?" Bear asked, as if to change the subject. "You wish to make meat?"

"Yes. We cannot keep killing our cattle for food."

"You come. I will show you where the hunting is good for both deer and elk."

"I'm much obliged, Bear."

He said something to Willow and Willow spoke to their son. I believe they were speaking Spanish. I heard the word *gusanos* and thought I might have heard that word before, down in Texas. A moment later, Turtle went into the tent and came out carrying a leather pouch that was round and had a hard bottom. He set it down and I looked into it. It was full of white grub worms. Turtle grinned at me and then his mother shooed him away. He picked up the bag and ran into the timber.

Then Willow did a surprising thing. She walked up to me and touched my shirt sleeve. She grabbed a piece of cloth with two fingers and felt it, then looked up into my face.

"You do not have the buckskins," she said.

"Ah, no, ma'am."

"You bring to Willow the hide of the deer or the elk and Willow will make for you the buckskins."

I looked over at Bear. He nodded, a faint smile on his lips.

"Yes'm, I'd like that," I said.

"You wear the buckskins," she said, "and you will be a man of the mountains. Very good medicine."

Then she slapped the sleeve of my shirt as if to tell me what I was wearing wasn't fit for a man living in the mountains.

Bear stood up and so did I.

"You will ride?" I asked.

"No, I will walk. You ride. There is a good place to hunt not far from here and you can make meat for your family."

I said good-bye to Willow. She did not wave, but nodded to me. Bear went inside the tent. When he emerged, he had something slung around his neck that was tied to a leather thong. It looked like a tube made out of hard dried leather. It dangled over his chest. It appeared to be a bunch of bull cocks all joined together with glue. There was something wooden sticking out of the top end of it where the thong was joined.

Bear started walking toward the edge of the meadow where we had come in and I got on Dan and followed him. Bear carried his Henry Yellow Boy and did not look back. He seemed to me a mystical figure in his buckskins, walking across the meadow, part of the earth, part of the grass and sky.

The place where Bear took me was an ideal spot, not far from where he was camped, but on higher ground. He led me to a rocky shelf overlooking a ravine where the trees had been thinned out by natural forces: lightning, floods, aging.

"Just below," he said, "there is a game trail. Deer and elk use this trail. If you sit here with that bush behind you, they cannot see or smell you if you do not move."

I tied my horse higher up, then walked back down to the rimrock shelf Bear had shown me. I sat down with bushes behind and on either side of me. I could see the game trail some thirty yards down the slope that fell off below where I sat.

Bear grunted with satisfaction.

"This is good. Do you know how to call the elk?"

I shook my head.

Bear took the cylindrical object from his neck and showed it to me.

"This is made from the cocks of buffalo bulls," he said.

"The skin has been dried and glued together. It is hollow inside. I carved this mouthpiece. You can blow into it and make the elk call. I will show you."

Bear held the instrument up and blew on it. The tube emitted a high-pitched shriek that was as clear as a note from a flute and then the sound descended the scale and ended in a kind of grunt.

"In the fall, when the bull elk calls, you can play this bugle and he will come to your rifle and you can shoot him. He will come very close if you make this sound like his own voice. I give this to you so you may practice until you are perfect."

"But I have never heard an elk call."

"You will. Soon, when the bulls begin to mate."

I took the elk call from Bear and thanked him. He did not say good-bye, but walked down from the precipice and disappeared into the trees. I sat there a long time examining the strange instrument he had given me. Then I slipped the thong over my neck and let the caller dangle over my chest as he had done.

Then I sat there on the rimrock and waited, watching the game trail below and peering upward at the blue sky and the wafting puffs of clouds floating over me toward the distant plain.

I thought of Nora and wished she could be there with me, taking in the awesome beauty of the mountains. It was very quiet and then I heard a jay in the distance. The jay was scolding something, a squirrel perhaps, yet I wondered if the bird was announcing my presence to the deer and the elk. I knew that the big clove-hoofed animals were probably bedded down and that I might have to wait all day until they started to move along the trail.

I held my rifle across my lap and listened to every sound, every silence.

A red-tailed hawk floated over the rimrock behind and

above me, its head moving from side to side as it sought food on the ground. I watched it flap its wings once, catch an air current and sail down into the evergreens. Then the jays began screeching again, a bunch of them this time and I wondered if they were chasing the hawk down in the woods below.

But I never saw a jay break the skyline above the trees. Soon it grew silent again and I stood up to stretch my legs. I walked around, keeping quiet, to restore circulation to my feet, which had been turning numb from sitting so long in one place.

I was beginning to think I wasn't going to see either deer or elk as the morning wore on and the temperature rose. I went back to my place of semi-concealment and sat down. I pulled the brim of my hat down to keep the sun out of my eyes and I waited, listening for any sound that might indicate an animal approaching along the game trail, a snapping twig, a cracking branch, a muffled footfall. But there was nothing and the sky above was empty of birds. Great white clouds began to drift over the far snowcapped peaks and float toward me. Perhaps, I thought, they will hide the sun for a while and bring some coolness by the middle of the day.

I was beginning to get drowsy when I heard a rustling somewhere down below me that made my senses sizzle like bacon frying in a pan. I held my breath and gripped my rifle, ready to bring it to my shoulder. A twig snapped.

The outcropping blocked my view, so I leaned over for a better look. There was more rustling as if some animal was walking through the small trees and brush, which spread out below the rimrock. Then there was movement. Leaves jiggled and another branch popped as if some large animal had stepped on a downed limb.

My heart pounded in my chest as if a wild bird were beating its wings inside the walls of my lungs. Still, I couldn't see what was making the noise, but I knew it had to be game and we needed meat.

I crawled back away from the ledge and stood up. I crept to a path leading down into the brush and the incessant phalanxes of pines that spread out in countless ranks for miles in every direction. I was very quiet and I was listening, too. The noises continued, making my heart pound even faster.

Below, I followed a path beneath the rimrock, trying not to make noise through the brush. There was a huge berry patch growing there, blackberries, I thought, and the brambles caught at my clothes, tugged at my trousers.

I stopped to listen after clearing one patch of berries and then realized my mistake.

There was something small and black ahead of me, thrashing through the bushes. Then there was another. The creatures made a lot of noise and I watched them for a few minutes, unsure of what they were.

I knew they weren't deer or elk. At first I thought they might be some mighty big groundhogs or some animal unknown to me that lived in the mountains.

Then the little creatures rolled down out of the brush and onto bare ground, a patch of earth that stood between the berries and the tall pines. The animals stood up and started to box at each other.

Then I recognized what they were from pictures I had seen in a book.

Bears. Bear cubs.

I had never seen a live bear before and the cubs were fascinating to watch.

A moment later, I heard something big crashing through the brush and then this big black bear stood up and looked straight at me.

My blood seemed to freeze in my veins as fear iced my innards, chilled the marrow in my spine. I was aware of sunlight and shadow and the big black bear's startling presence not thirty yards away, its small close-set eyes glaring at me like pulsing coals in a fire. I could smell the bear. Its musk was overpowering, a stench of death and decay as if it had been wallowing in carrion. Its mouth opened and I saw its huge teeth, the redness of its tongue. I could almost feel its fetid breath blowing hot against my face. My legs were quivering and seemed rooted to the ground.

Then I heard a terrifying roar behind me. I jerked my head at the sound and saw another black bear, an even larger one, standing next to a tree some twenty yards behind me, its head uplifted, its jaws open wide, its teeth stained with berry juice that looked like blood.

My movement evidently angered the nearest bear because it roared again and charged at me, dropping to all fours and bounding through the bushes with a speed that surprised me. At the same time, the other bear growled and, snarling, loped toward me, as well.

I yelled and ran toward the cliff, then realized I would be trapped there. Both bears were growling and snarling and I knew there was little chance I could outrun them. But I ran along the cliff wall and then turned to go downhill. I tripped on a bush and fell face forward.

When I scrambled to my feet, the larger bear was upon me. It stood up on its hind legs and walked toward me, a bellowing roar issuing from its throat. Then it swiped a massive paw at me. I ducked, but its claws raked across the top of my head and I felt blood gush from my scalp and stream down my face.

Blinded, I turned to run away and ran into the smaller bear. It clasped me in its arms and I could feel the breath burning in my lungs, unable to escape through my mouth.

Hot breath scalded my face and the sky spun around as

the bear bent me over backward, its jaws opening to bite me in the face.

I screamed in terror.

I knew right then that I was about to die a horrible death. I felt sharp claws tear my shirt and dig into my back.

I closed my eyes, hoping that my death would be quick.

16

WHAT IS IT IN A MAN THAT RISES UP IN TIMES OF DANGER AND transforms him from a powerless weakling into a powerful savage? What mental alchemy is present when a man faces certain death, yet manages to find some core of strength beyond himself, some hidden faculty that enables him to quell that paralyzing fear in his belly, that terror that constricts his throat and renders him mute and defenseless, and find the courage and the determination to live when death is staring him in the face?

I did not know, but something way back in a far dark corner of my brain shouted to me that I must not give up, nor fall down, nor let myself be devoured or mutilated by a bear with long teeth and bad breath.

I ducked and whirled, and rammed the butt of my Winchester into the larger bear's throat as hard as I could, with a strength I had never owned before. I heard a crunch and felt soft fur give way to fragile bone. The bear slammed a paw with sharp claws into my side and raked away my shirt and portions of flesh. The pain in my side was searing, as if someone had ravaged me with the tines of a rake heated in a fire. I staggered away, spun out of the bear's reach by the force of its blow.

The smaller bear loomed nearby and I prepared to defend myself against it even as I grew dizzy and disoriented. Blood streaked down my side and soaked my trousers. I could feel its warmth and wetness and thought that there must be a hole in me as large as a skillet.

I stumbled on rocks beneath my feet and tried to bring my rifle up to a shooting position. But, the small bear swiped the barrel aside and then, roaring, rushed past me, its porcine eyes flashing with a visible rage. Still, I hung onto my rifle and staggered farther along the rock wall, descending into brush. The smaller bear waded into the big bear and, snarling and clawing, tried to bite the larger bear's neck. To my surprise, what I took to be the mother of the cubs attacked the big bear with such a fury that she drove the he-bear back against the bluff.

I ran downhill, past the two cubs which were frightened and trying to climb a tree. It was then that I heard Dan's frantic whinny, so high-pitched that it was like a woman's scream. And I realized that Dan had been whinnying like that ever since the first bear had roared at me. In my fear, I had submerged the sound so that it just didn't register in my scrambled brain.

"Dan," I yelled, as I stumbled downhill, gravity pulling me faster and faster. Up on the rimrock, I heard Dan's shod hooves clattering like iron hammers on flat stone.

The two bears were still at it, growling, roaring, snarling, flailing at each other, their heads bobbing and weaving like boxers in the final seconds of a round. I looked up and saw Dan pacing back and forth, jerking the reins, trying to break free of the place where I had tied him.

I kept running straight downhill until I reached flat ground, where I changed direction, hoping to circle the place where the bears were fighting and get to high ground where I could defend myself with my rifle.

I charged right through openings in the trees, thinking that I might be able to get back up on the ledge where I had tied Dan. As I came out into a small meadow, I had a good view of the outcropping. I stopped, waved my arms and called out again to Dan. He bunched his muscles, backed up, and broke free of the tie-down bush. He galloped along the ledge, jumped over a boulder, and was soon on grassy ground. I kept calling to him. I could see the bears grappling and hear them snarling. The cubs were halfway up a tree, looking like frightened kittens, hanging on for dear life.

I ran to meet Dan as he came galloping up, reins trailing. I grabbed the reins and pulled him to a stop. I patted his neck and rubbed his withers, speaking to him in a soothing tone of voice.

"Good boy," I said. "Just stay steady, boy. We're going to get the hell out of here."

When Dan was calmed down, I mounted him, and drew my first deep breath in a long while. The female bear won the scrap. I saw the he-bear amble off in the opposite direction, grumbling as he loped away on all fours. The mother bear dropped to the ground and went to rescue her cubs. I let out a sigh of relief. Then I felt my side and looked down to see the claw marks. They were seeping blood. My head hurt and I felt my scalp and forehead. My hand came away bloody.

As I climbed up into the saddle, I realized I was trembling all over. My legs quivered so that my foot made the stirrup sway. I pulled myself into the saddle and it felt almost like home when I settled down in its leather cradle. I felt safe, out of harm's way. But I also felt like a coward, wanting to run away from danger, and worse, using a horse to wage my inner battle. The tremors in my hands increased as if I were in the grip of buck fever. I had to steady them on the saddlehorn, the palsy was so pronounced.

I sat there, breathing in and out, trying to calm myself. I lifted one hand and touched Dan on the neck. He, too, was quivering, and his ears twisted back and forth as the mother bear and her cubs crashed through the berry patch, scrambling to get away from the male, which was standing up, clawing a tree with its paws, a raspy sound coming from its damaged throat.

Finally, I managed to align my senses and realize that I did not have the sand to hunt for deer or elk. I wanted only to ride home and wipe away the memory of this place, a place where I had come very close to losing my life.

I turned Dan and headed further downslope, thinking to make a wide circle away from the bluffs and find a trail leading back to our homestead. Dan seemed eager to make tracks, too, and he stepped out in lively fashion, weaving his way through the pines and stepping over deadfalls, avoiding brush tangles. I kept my eyes on the skyline and made for home by dead reckoning. We found another narrow game trail, or sheep path, and then started climbing. I could see the top of Ute Mountain off to my left and knew that I was on course for home.

17

MOTHER MADE A BIG FUSS OVER ME WHEN DAN AND I GOT
back home. She washed my scratches and salved them,
wrapped my waist with cloth bandages she made from feed
sacks she had saved and washed. I was glad that Luke and
Pa weren't there. I was still shaking inside for a long time
after I unsaddled Dan and put him up to feed. Ma made me
some broth and made me drink the entire bowl.

"You stay away from those bears, Chip, you hear?" she
said.

"I plan to. I feel bad that I didn't bring any meat home,
though."

"We're not lacking," she said and I began to feel better.
But she made me lie down on my cot and stay still the rest
of the day.

"I want those wounds to scab over," she told me. "Otherwise, you'll be bleeding for a week."

"Yes'm," I said, and slept until Pa and Luke got back
from the valley. Of course my mother told them all about

my close call with the wild bears and Luke gave me a funny
look, but he didn't say anything.

That night, as if to spite me, Luke shot a fat mule deer
that came close to the cabin to investigate. When he was
skinning it out, I asked him for the hide and told him about
meeting the Ute family. I was surprised at his reaction. Pa's
too. I thought they'd be glad that I had made some friends.

"You ever think that Ute put you down there where the
bears were on purpose?" Luke asked.

"No, I never thought that. I don't think he did."

"Well, it's mighty funny that the Ute's name is Bear and
you got torn up by a real bear. Them Injuns put a lot of
store in totems and such."

"I wouldn't put it past them," Pa said. "Treacherous
savages."

"They were right friendly, Pa."

He snorted. Luke skinned out the deer and gave me the
hide. I put it in a sack, meaning to scrape it and take it to
Willow.

"You'll need more than one deerskin if that squaw's
goin' to make you some buckskins," Luke said. "You got to
soak it in lye water, get all the hair off, too."

"She just told me to bring her the hide. I'll get a deer
yet. Or maybe an elk," I told Luke.

"With your luck, Chip, we may be tannin' your hide
next time you go out huntin'."

"Very funny, Luke. You ought to be on the stage—the
stage out of town."

I took Luke's ribbing as good natured banter, which of
course it was. That's just the way Luke was. He had a cyn-
ical eye, after all he'd been through in life and I was used to
the way he looked at things.

As it turned out, I didn't have to take the deer hide to
Bear's wife. The next day, all three of them, Bear, Willow,

and Turtle, turned up at our cabin real early in the morning. I introduced everyone, including my father who was all sulled up like a raincloud that morning for some reason. He sniffed Bear as if the Ute was something drug in by a stray dog. I couldn't blame him much, though. To my father, an Indian was an Indian and he made no distinction between Ute and Comanche.

Willow brought my mother some blackberries she said she had picked a month ago and dried in the sun so they'd keep.

"Why, that's very nice of you, Willow," my mother said.

"You can mix them in the meat and dry the meat," Willow said. "Good food."

My father was wary of Bear, but they shook hands.

"Did you see what that bear did to my son, Chip, there?" Pa said. I was still wrapped in Ma's bandage and reeked of salve.

Bear looked at me, a puzzled expression on his face.

"You saw a bear?" the Ute said.

"Two big ones and two little ones. The big one clawed me in the side."

"Ah, the cubs. The mother bear might have wanted to kill you. They do not like people around their cubs."

"She attacked the big bear, too."

"Even the he-bear. When there are cubs, the mother will fight."

"Did you come up here to talk about bears?" Pa asked. He was blunt, I thought. And rude. My mother wore a look of infinite patience on her face, a look I had seen many times before.

"I did not know about the bears and your son," Bear said. "We pass this way because we go to the valley beyond La Ventana." Bear lifted his arm and pointed toward the "window" in the rocky ridge some miles from us. "We go there to catch the wild horses. There may be a council there. There was smoke in the sky saying this."

"A war council?" My father looked as if he were getting his dander up. He positively bristled.

Bear shrugged. "Maybe. I do not know. We go there to catch horses for the trading. We do this every year. Catch the horses, take them to Taos to trade. What our people call 'magic dogs.' We go to Taos after the Moon of the Falling Leaves."

"If the Utes make war, will you fight with them?" Pa was nothing if not persistent.

"If the tribe makes war with the white eyes, then me and my family, we will have a council, too, I think." Bear was smiling when he said it, but I could see that my father did not see the humor in it.

My mother was admiring Willow's buckskin dress. She made a big fuss over the beadwork. I saw Willow smiling as she explained what the various patterns and symbols meant. My father still had his dander up, like a dog with the hackles raised on the back of its neck. Luke wandered over to a log that had been flatted on one side with an axe. That was the workbench he was using to make furniture for the cabin. It looked to me as if he wanted to put some distance between himself, my father, and Bear in case a fight broke out.

"If you're not in any hurry," Mercy said to Bear, "let me fix you breakfast. I was going to make flapjacks if that's to your liking."

"You have the syrup?" Bear asked.

"We have syrup and sugar for your coffee if you fancy to break your fast with us."

Bear grinned. That moon face of his lit up at the mention of syrup and sugar. Willow, too, smiled, and when I glanced down at Turtle, he had a grin on his face that was almost as bright as the rising sun.

While my mother prepared our breakfast, with Willow looking on, little Turtle roamed around the cabin, examining it both inside and out. Bear sat down with my father, Luke, and me, brought out his pipe, filled the bowl with tobacco and lit it. He passed the pipe around after offering the smoke to the four directions. To my surprise, my father smoked it, and so did Luke. Again, I choked on the smoke before I handed the pipe back to Bear.

"We smoke," Bear said, "to show that we are friends, that we breathe the same air, that our spirits are all alike."

"I wish the Comanches had done some smoking instead of scalping," Pa said. "But I never felt no kin to them, either in spirit or body."

"Me, neither," Luke said.

I was fascinated with Bear and I watched him as he spoke. I also noticed the look on my father's face as he listened to the Ute.

"We are seven tribes," Bear said. "I am of the Capote tribe. Since the white eyes made reservations, we are all few, all of the tribes are small and scattered. These will not live on the reservation in Denver."

"Why not?" Pa asked.

"We were always free. We wish to be free now. We are not cattle to be put in pens."

We ate while Bear explained that a man named Sobotar was the true Chief of the Capote Utes, but that his father, Umiya, had split off from that tribe to follow his own path. He said that his people had once traded peacefully with the Spaniards who had changed their lives when they gave the Utes some of their magic dogs, their horses. Ever since then, he said, the tribes had broken up into smaller groups and even the main tribes had broken up.

"It sounds like a mess," Luke said.

"We are still the same people," Bear said.

"It don't sound like it to me," Pa said. "You don't own any land and you don't have any rights."

"We never did own land," Bear said. "The land belongs to the Great Spirit. We are only those who watch over it."

Pa snorted.

When the meal was over, Bear and his family thanked my mother and said good-bye.

Before he left, though, Bear asked my father if he had found the grave yet.

"What grave?"

Bear pointed to a place at the far edge of the shelf where our cabin stood. There was a stand of trees there and some rocks.

"That is where a woman and her two daughters are buried," Bear said.

"Under those rocks?" Pa said.

Bear nodded.

"Who were they?" Ma asked. "How did they die?"

"They were Mexicans who lived here. I do not know their names. The woman was the wife of a man who herded the sheep here in the summer. Her two daughters were also killed."

"Killed?" my mother said.

"The husband desecrated the sacred things on Ute Mountain. The Muache Utes heard of this and they came here and killed those three. The husband did not die, but he never returned. The Muaches took away all his sheep and they ate them over many winters and summers."

"How horrible," Ma said.

"The Mexicans did not respect the sacred things of the Ute," Bear said.

"Are you warning us?" Pa asked.

Bear walked away, followed by Willow and Turtle.

"The grave there is your warning," he said, and then disappeared over the edge of the precipice.

I looked at my mother. Her face was drawn and the color drained from it.

My father clenched his fists and glared in the direction where the Utes had gone. I prayed that he would not yell out at them and cause me embarrassment.

"Threaten me, will he?" my father muttered under his breath.

"Keith, he wasn't threatening you," my mother said.

"Sure as hell sounded like a threat to me," Luke said, kicking at the ground with the toe of his boot.

I wanted to run after Bear and tell him that I wanted always to be his friend. But I knew if I did that, I could never come back home again.

Hatreds among people die slow, and my father, I realized, was on the verge of hating the Utes as much as he had hated the Comanches.

Luke was already in that blind place where he had chosen to be.

18

In the days that followed the visit from Bear and his family, I spent more and more time away from our cabin. I hunted and explored, venturing far from the promontory above the valley, riding Dan into places of beauty, mystery, and wonder. I shot my first deer one day and took the carcass back home, dressed it out, then left the next day. Luke said he'd take care of the hide for me. Mother was glad to see me, and I noticed that she had made the cabin very homey, putting up curtains that she had sewed, arranging the furniture my father and Luke had built. Yet the days of summer were racing by and I knew we would have to leave the mountains before the first snows flew. I sensed a sadness in my mother when she talked about leaving that place she made into a home.

"I wish we could spend the whole year up here," she said. "I will feel like a gypsy when we have to leave."

"Mother," I said, "the snows up here would bury the cabin and us in it. Selva said no one could survive a winter at this altitude."

"I know," she said, and there was a wistful look on her face, a sadness that came out in a long sigh of resignation.

Sometime in August, I figured about the middle, the elk began bugling. At first, I didn't know what it was, but Luke said that haunting, flute-like sound signified that the bulls were in the rut. I stood outside in the dusk every evening and listened to the bugling in the hills and valleys around our homestead. I began to practice bugling with the call that Bear had given me. At first, I could not imitate the sound of the bull elk, but after some days, I began to achieve a sonorous replication of the calls. When I rode off each day to hunt, I looked for a likely place to sit and call in elk.

At first, I had no luck in calling elk. But I found out how to bring the bugling elk to my gun. It was simple, really. When I heard a young bull bugling, I imitated its call exactly. I did not call too much, but just enough to challenge the elk I was calling. I learned to listen to the change in the bugling that told me the elk was coming closer to my concealed stand.

One day, perhaps early in September, I called in an elk. I heard him first, then saw him, drifting through the pines like a brown ghost, his huge antlers plainly visible. What a majestic animal, I thought, a kingly stag in a king's private forest.

I sat very still, unmoving, my back against a large pine so that I had no silhouette. The elk stopped, turned its head, its antlers sweeping like a leafless tree in the wind. I bugled softly and ended the call with a grunt. The elk stared directly at me, its nostrils quivering to pick up my scent. But the wind was blowing in my direction.

The elk came within twenty yards of me and my heart began pounding so loudly I was sure the animal could hear it. The elk, with its large brown eyes, stood motionless, its gaze locked on mine. I did not blink. I did not breathe. I sat there, quaking inside with the thrill of seeing the animal so close. I knew that if I moved, the elk would bound away in a twinkling.

I wanted to shoot it, yet I also wanted it to live, to go on breathing and displaying its royal set of antlers, its perfectly formed body with its muscles all in perfect tune.

The elk snorted. It pawed the ground. Then it lifted its head and bugled. The sound sent a thrill through me such as I'd never experienced before. The notes were all pure and elegantly simple, yet they seemed to harken back to some primitive melody from ancient times. It was the sound of a hunting horn and the melodic phrases from the god, Pan. The music rippled through me and I sat there, transfixed, lost in its magic, mesmerized by its haunting and plaintive harmonics.

Entranced, I watched the sunlight spray through the trees leaving dappled shadows on the elk's back and side, shadows that shifted and changed shape and seemed as much a part of the bull's coat as the sunlight. The elk waited, turned its head and gazed off into trees. Then I saw them, a line of elk coming toward the bull in single file, a procession of brown bodies gliding through the timber. The elk were all sizes and ages.

My heart pumped fast and the tremors began rippling in my hands, traveled up my arms like spasms from a heatless fever.

I did not want to shoot the bull. He was too beautiful to destroy. Instead, I picked out a younger animal, a bull much smaller, without antlers, perhaps a year or two old, slightly larger than a large mule deer. I did not want to kill a cow, either. So I picked out the young bull and tried to quell my attack of buck fever.

Nature itself took the decision out of my hands. A wood tick landed on my hand and started scratching a path toward my sleeve. It had a little white spot on its back and its legs moved fast. That jarred me out of my feverish state. I dove a hand down at it to pluck it off or flick it away. That movement caught the eye of the bull elk and he snorted. The moving herd of elk stopped and every eye looked my way.

I brushed away the tick and brought my rifle up slowly. The yearling bull was no more than thirty yards from me when I pulled the butt of my rifle into my shoulder and eased back the hammer. I took a deep breath and held it. My tremors vanished. Then the herd bull saw me and turned to run away. The other elk reacted in a flash, all their heads came up with necks stretched and then they bolted. I dropped the front blade sight on the young bull and followed him with the barrel as he dashed away on my side of the herd, out in the open. I lined up the rear buckhorn and tracked his speed and direction. As the muzzle caught up to the bull, I followed through with my lead and squeezed the trigger, my breath burning in my lungs. The rifle barked and the stock bucked against my shoulder. The report echoed for a long time. Through the smoke I saw the elk jump as the bullet struck him just behind its left front leg where it joined his body.

The yearling stumbled, fell, got up and then ran for some distance as the herd scattered, their hoofbeats rumbling as they galloped away, breaking twigs, cracking limbs. Finally, there was a silence that grew up around me. I jacked another cartridge into the chamber of my Winchester, took a deep breath, and got up to track the wounded elk.

There was a good blood trail. There was blood mixed with white froth and I saw pieces of windpipe on the ground. It was a lung shot, but I wondered if I had hit the elk's heart. I found the animal, dead, about 150 yards away from where I had shot it, its eyes glazed and glistening like wet glass, its tongue caught between its teeth as if gripped in its death throes.

I knelt down beside it, panting from excitement and exertion. I touched its hide, felt the heat of its body. It was bigger than any deer I had ever shot. I laid my rifle down nearby and drew my knife. Slowly, carefully, I gutted the elk out, removed its heart. The bullet had torn a piece of it away and severed an artery. It amazed me that the animal had been able to run that far after being mortally wounded.

I had been told that animals don't feel pain after they've been shot, but I didn't believe that. At least this one had not suffered long. I removed the entrails, tucked the heart and liver inside my shirt, and walked back with my rifle to get Dan. When I returned, I heaved the dead elk up on the saddle and rope-tied it securely. I would walk back to the cabin, leading Dan, thinking about the whole experience, wondering as I always did at such times, about life and death.

It was a hard climb back to the cabin, but it gave me time to think. I stopped often to look back down at the huge valley and the mountains rising above it all in green and flowing with a vibrant energy. I thought of Nora and how much she would have loved views like these. I still missed her and still thought of her a lot, dreamed of her at night.

I wondered if she could see me from wherever she was. I wondered if she could know what was in my heart. I wondered if she missed me as I missed her.

I had to stop thinking about her because I was ready to cry at times.

I had killed my first elk.

That rifle shot still echoed in my mind, sounding like a bullwhip cracking in the silence of this mountain fastness. It seemed to me that I had subtracted something from the beauty that surrounded me. There was an emptiness that rose up in me and put a hollowness in the pit of my stomach.

I wondered if there was something wrong with me. I

should have felt pride in downing an elk, at bringing home food for my family and for Luke. But I was gripped with a cloying sadness that I couldn't explain. It was not a good feeling.

I wondered if my feelings had anything to do with being a coward at heart.

Maybe the high altitude added to my confusion, but by the time I got back home with my elk, I was sullen and downspirited. Luke clapped me on the back and congratulated me. Pa grunted his approval and Ma beamed at me as I reached into my shirt pocket and handed her the heart and liver which were still warm.

I just wanted to be alone with my thoughts and my worry whether or not I was a coward, a misfit in a world where man killed to eat and fought to live free.

I wondered if I could ever kill another living thing.

I wondered if I could ever kill a man.

19

THE ASPEN LEAVES TURNED YELLOW AND WE SAW WILD GEESE in the sky, flying south in long graceful vees, heard their sonorous honking from our cabin on the edge of the world. There was a decided chill in the air, even during the daytime, and we knew it was time to drive the cattle down out of the high country and take up winter quarters.

It was difficult to leave that place that we had come to call home. It had been an idyllic summer for me, even though I was lonesome for Nora and missed some of the neighbors we'd had in Texas. But I had learned much and seen a lot of beautiful country. I wondered just how hard it could be to spend a winter in the mountains above ten thousand feet.

"Damned hard," Luke told me when we were rounding up strays, running them into the main herd.

"How do you know?"

"Heard tell," was all he said.

Later, after Luke and I had finished, and left Pa to watch the herd, we rode up to the cabin to help Ma load the wagon with our goods. She was still packing, but she had some things set aside.

"Luke, you and Chip ride up to that Ute shrine, will you? I've set aside some things to leave there."

Luke's face darkened like a rain cloud, but he didn't say anything.

Ma pointed to a keg chair. She had set out a pretty blue scarf, a beaded necklace made of red-colored glass, and a little coin purse.

"I put a fifty-cent piece in that purse. You boys leave it be when you take it up," Ma said.

"I really ought to be helpin' Keith with that herd," Luke said. "They might get restless."

"No, you go on up with Chip. I saw smoke a little while ago. Better to be safe than sorry."

"Smoke?" I asked. "You mean smoke signals?"

"That's right," she said, a bit too cheerily, I thought.

"Where?"

"Coming from over yonder beyond La Ventana."

"Something must be up," Luke said.

"Probably just talking about us, Luke," I said. "Us leaving and all."

"Well, shoot," Luke said.

I stuffed the goods Ma gave me inside my shirt and Luke and I rode up through the trees to the shelf that bordered Ute Mountain. I could tell he was in a sullen mood because he griped at every tree branch that brushed against his face or pine needle that whacked him across the mouth.

"What's eating you, Luke?" I asked when we climbed up onto the plateau.

"I wish I was in Texas," he said.

"Why? Don't you like the mountains?"

"I want to put my boots on ground that I won't fall off of. I'm tired of riding at a tilt. I hate trees."

"Boy, you got a bad case of the grumps, Luke."

"You've heard of cabin fever? Well, I got mountain fever. I get the headaches and the air's so damned thin you can't hardly breathe it unless it's got smoke in it. You can't see more'n five feet in any direction once you get among all these trees. Findin' stray cattle is like lookin' for a needle in a stack of needles."

"Well, I like it up here."

"Chip," he started to say, then looked at me sharply. "Chip. Where'd you get that name, anyways?"

"Luke, you've been knowing me all this time and are just now getting to ask me about my name?"

"I know it ain't your real name. What's it say in your family Bible? I bet it don't say 'Chip.'"

"No, I got that nickname when I was a kid, about seven I guess. I fell and broke off the tip of my front tooth. Pa and Ma started calling me Chip and the name stuck."

"So, what's your real name?"

I laughed.

"What's so funny?" he said.

"It's been so long since I've been called by my real name, I near forgot it. I carried that chip in my tooth until I grew a new one. I guess I looked pretty goofy."

"So, what's your real name?" Luke asked again.

"Barr."

"Barr?"

"With two r's in it. Named after my uncle, who died young."

"Never heard a name like that."

"Well, you can call me Chip. Like always."

Luke kept saying "Barr" over and over, just under his breath, until we reached the shrine. I was about to dismount and put the things there, when Luke reached over and held my arm.

"Give 'em to me," he said. "I'll put 'em there. 'Sides, I got to take a pee."

I reached inside my shirt and slipped the items out, handed them to Luke.

"You just sit tight," he said, and dismounted. He walked over to the shrine. To my surprise, he opened the coin purse, took out the coin, and put it in his pocket. Then he laid the other items on the shelf with the other artifacts that had been left there before.

Luke then unbuttoned his fly. He moved up close and sprayed everything that was there on that shrine. He must have held his pee for a long time because there was plenty of it. When he finished, he shook himself off, put his pecker back in his pants, and buttoned them up. He leaned down and picked up a handful of dirt, washed his hands, brushed them on his pants.

He climbed back on his horse and looked at me.

"That's what I think of that danged shrine," he said.

"You stole money, Luke."

"Where in hell's a damned Injun gonna spend four bits?"

"It's still stealing."

"You gonna arrest me, Chip?"

"I think you made a mistake. You defiled a sacred place."

"Sacred to who? The redskins? Savages. Come on, let's get the hell out of here."

I rode back to the cabin in a state of numbness. I had discovered that my idol had feet of clay. I had always looked up to Luke, ever since he had come to work for us. But now I saw him in a different light. He was no longer the man of character, but only someone small and petty, who harbored hatred and resentments, who didn't care for the feelings of others. I had the feeling he had undone all the good things my father and mother had done. My parents had respected the Utes and their sacred mountain. Luke had not only stolen from the Utes, but from my mother, as well. By taking that fifty-cent piece, he had shown me someone shallow, disrespectful, and inconsiderate of others.

I wondered if any Utes had seen us. Perhaps one or more of them had watched as Luke desecrated their shrine. I looked up, scanned the top of Ute Mountain, the ridge running opposite it. It seemed to me that I saw movement on that opposite ridge, but I couldn't be sure.

Then I saw a man stand up and wave a blanket. A moment later, there was a puff of smoke. I reined up Dan and called out to Luke.

"Luke, hold up. Looky yonder." I pointed to the ridge. Three small puffs of smoke rose in the air.

"So?"

"Whoever is up there saw you pee on that shrine, Luke."

"The hell with them."

I heard noises from the valley where Pa was minding the cattle.

"Listen," I said.

Luke stopped his horse then, and cocked his head in the direction we were riding. His horse's ears stood up straight and twisted in a half-circle. Dan's ears did the same.

We both heard it then, the high-pitched yelps. A scream that I was sure was my mother's. Then the faint sound of hundreds of hoofbeats.

"Those are war cries," Luke said, and his voice sounded funny, low and gravelly in his throat.

My arms crawled with chills that raised and stiffened the hairs on them. I felt a queasiness boiling in my stomach.

We both heard the woman's scream again, so faint from that distance, but no mistaking from where it was coming.

"That's my mother," I croaked.

Luke started to shake his head in denial, but he never got that far.

We both turned at another sound from off to our left,

across the flat. There, at the foot of Ute Mountain, coming through the gap between there and the opposite ridge, a pack of nearly naked Utes rode toward us on small painted ponies. Their wild yips filled the air.

"Into the trees," Luke said. "Take cover."

My thoughts were racing, but I followed Luke off the shelf and we dropped into the thick woods. He quickly dismounted and tied his horse to a sturdy bush. He jerked his rifle from its scabbard and took up a position at the top of the slope facing the oncoming riders.

I leaped from Dan and tied him to another bush, grabbed my rifle and slid in beside Luke.

"They're running off our cattle," Luke said.

"That was my mother screaming," I said, badly rattled at all that was happening. I couldn't sort it all out. My senses were scrambled and fear turned my stomach to cold iron before it melted and sent cold shivers all through me.

"Here they come," Luke said, cocking the lever on his rifle. I heard the mechanism move and the cartridge slide up into the firing chamber.

The Utes charged straight toward us, in a bunch. Then, when they were two hundred yards away, they fanned out. I counted seven of them, then saw another horse separate.

There were eight Utes coming to kill us. They had feathers in their hair and their faces were painted. They carried bows and arrows. Just before they came into range, they bent over and hugged their horses so that we could barely see them. The hairs on the back of my neck stood up and my scalp rippled with spidery tingles as cold as ice.

"Let's give 'em what for," Luke muttered.

The Utes galloped still closer, then, as if they were one, they each sat straight and pulled their bows back. Each one had an arrow nocked to the string.

Their ponies started to zigzag and I tried to bring my sights down on the nearest brave.

Before I could pull the trigger, I saw one Ute release his arrow. Then two of the others shot their arrows. I ducked when I saw an arrow flying straight toward me in a high arc.

Luke touched his trigger and his rifle fired. The blow-back peppered my cheek with hot powder.

The first arrow whiffled toward me with a swishing sound.

In that instant, I knew that Luke and I were surely going to die.

20

LUKE'S BULLET STRUCK THE LEAD UTE SQUARE IN THE CHEST just as an arrow whizzed past my ear and three more stabbed the ground in front of us. The Ute threw up his arms. His bow went flying as he tumbled from the bare back of his pony. He hit the ground with a loud thud and skidded a dozen feet before crumpling up into a heap. I fired my rifle at a Ute that started to veer off and flank us. I saw the man twitch as my bullet burrowed into his side. Blood sprayed out the other side and he toppled from his pinto.

Luke fired again and again, through the smoke, and I saw ponies go down, men's arms and legs flailing. He was a good shot. The remaining Utes turned their ponies around and galloped away, their bodies sliding off to the opposite side of their mounts so that we could not see them.

I fired at the ponies and missed. I kept moving the lever until my rifle was empty and then it took me a couple of seconds before I realized the firing pin was hitting on an empty chamber. I was out of breath and panting, my nerves jangling like a sackful of bells. My heart was pounding fast.

I saw dead Utes out there, but I was still afraid of them, afraid they might rise to their feet and shoot an arrow into my head. I slumped over my empty rifle and began to shake.

"Better cram some more cartridges in that Winchester, Chip," Luke said, and his voice jarred me out of my almost senseless state. I fished in my pockets for more .44/40 cartridges and slid them into the magazine with trembling fingers.

"They ain't comin' back," Luke said.

"Huh?"

"They rode on down through the woods, down toward the valley. I reckon they'll join up with the ones chasin' our cattle."

"Yeah."

"You got one. I got two. The rest got away."

"I-I never killed anybody before, Luke."

"There's a first time for everything, Chip."

I felt like strangling Luke. In my heart, I knew he had brought all this on us, as surely as if he had called down the Utes with verbal insults. But I kept my notions to myself since I had other matters on my mind. Those screams. My mother's screams.

"I'm going down to the cabin, Luke. I think my mother's in trouble. I'm sure I heard her screaming."

"I'll go with you, but keep your eyes peeled. We're outnumbered, for sure."

I grabbed up Dan's reins, untied him, and climbed into the saddle. I rode straight down the slope toward our cabin, weaving in and out of the trees. Luke kept up with me on a different course. We saw no Indians, and, in fact, it was so quiet, it was eerie. It was as if every bird, elk, deer, porcupine, and crow had just vanished.

When we got to the promontory, we both looked down into the valley. The cattle were still bunched, but we could tell that several, maybe twenty head, were missing. I scanned the opposite slope and saw something that brought my anger rising up inside me like my blood was boiling.

There were the missing cattle. They were being driven by at least a dozen Utes. They were heading straight for La Ventana. My blood ran cold a moment later when I saw my father, his hands bound behind him, riding between two Utes, with one in front and one behind so that he could not escape. His head hung down to his chest and I knew he was hurt, just by looking at him.

"Damn," Luke said. "They got Keith."

"Do you see my mother?"

Luke shook his head.

I dug spurs into Dan's flanks and raced down to the flat-iron where our cabin stood. I dismounted before Dan had stopped and hit the ground running. The front door was open. I raced inside, my heart clogged up somewhere in my throat. Then my heart just stopped.

Nothing in my life prepared me for the horror of that moment. It was beyond imagination, beyond any nightmare I'd ever had. I can only describe that instant as a great shock, not only to my senses, but to my heart, my very being.

My mother lay on the floor in the center of the room, bathed in her own blood. At first I thought she was dead, but she was moving, struggling to rise, but too weak to even lift her head.

Choking with a sudden gush of tears, I stumbled toward her, knelt down and grabbed her hand, clasped it tightly. Her eyes opened and closed. She tried to speak, but she was even too weak to do that. I knew she was in mortal pain and I thought she might be dying before my eyes.

"Ma," I gasped.

"Chip," she breathed. "Help me."

She was completely naked. Both of her breasts had been sliced off. Only ragged pieces of flesh remained at the edges of the circles where her breasts had been. There were bruises on her face where she had been struck. Both of her eyes were puffy and there were welts on her cheekbones.

I took off my shirt and covered as much of her as I could.

"Water," she croaked.

I nodded, stricken dumb by the horror of seeing her body so mutilated.

It was difficult to leave her, even for a moment, but I went into the kitchen and poured a glass of water from a pitcher. I passed by her bunk and grabbed a blanket so that I could cover her more completely. I also snatched up a towel that was hanging from a dowel on the wall.

"Here, Ma," I said, offering her the glass of water. I cradled her head in one arm and lifted it. She opened her lips and I tipped the glass. The water seeped into her mouth. When she had enough, which wasn't very much, she turned her head away and I let her head back down on the floor very gently. I removed my shirt and covered her with the blanket.

"I'm going to wash away the blood, Mother."

Her eyes closed and the lids tightened like tiny fists.

I knew she was in pain.

"Where's Keith?"

"He-he's alive, Ma. You be still now. I'm going to take care of you."

I poured some water on the towel and began wiping the blood from her neck. I lifted the blanket and wiped around the two wounds on her chest and then tried to clean her tummy, her legs. She winced every time I touched her and it pained me to hurt her.

"Powders," she said. Her voice was very faint, just barely above a whisper.

I knew what she meant. We had powders that were for pain, but I knew they wouldn't be of much use. I thought of all the medicants we had, the salves, tonics, powders, and

such we had brought from Texas. I also knew I couldn't
leave her lying on the floor like that.

"I'm going to put you in your bed, Ma."

She didn't answer.

I lifted her gently and carried her into the bedroom. I
lay her on her bed and told her I'd be right back. I moved
as if I were in a trance, giving thanks that she was still
alive, but cringing every time I thought of what the Utes
had done to her.

It wasn't a bedroom such as we had in Texas. Pa had put
up some poles as dividers and tacked blankets to them for
some modicum of privacy. He had made a nightstand. I
soon had a pitcher of water and a glass set on that. Then I
went through the medicine chest and rummaged among the
jars and tins and boxes until I found some that might help
my mother.

"Get your father," she whispered when I mixed the powders in the glass of water and held it up to her mouth.

"I will, Ma. Just take these powders for your pain." I
hoped she could not tell, in her state, that I was lying.

We might never see Pa again. I knew that. But I didn't
want her to know.

"No chance," she said. "They came . . . came right in."

"Please don't try to talk, Ma. I know. I'm going to take
care of you. You need to rest after I rub some salve on you.
On where . . ."

I couldn't say it. I don't know if my mother knew that her
breasts were gone. She was in a worse state of shock than I
was. Her eyes were cloudy with pain. I still had to bathe her
more completely and make sure she was comfortable.

I rubbed salve on her chest wounds as gently as I could
and felt my mother's cheeks to see if she was building a
fever. She was. I told her to sleep and then left the room,
wondering what else I could do. There was still the danger
of another attack.

Also, I was wondering why they had taken my father prisoner and not my mother. Why had they tortured her and left her alive? As hard as I tried I could not fathom the savage mind. For one human being to do something like this to another was beyond my comprehension.

Luke was standing outside, staring off toward La Ventana, his rifle in his hand.

"Them what jumped us," he said, "came back and got their dead. There they go yonder."

I looked up and saw the three dead Utes tied to their ponies. The others were following the same trail as those who had rustled our cattle and captured my father.

"I wonder if they'll be back," I said.

"One thing sure. We've got to get those cattle down to the flat and bring some help up here."

"You're going to have to do that all by yourself, Luke."

"Huh?"

"My mother's hurt real bad. She's alive, but just barely." Luke looked stricken.

"I thought she might be dead," he said. "When you went in there, I thought you'd find her dead."

"They mutilated her."

"Bad?"

"Very bad. They cut off her breasts, Luke. She's lost a lot of blood."

He swore under his breath.

"Anything I can do?" he asked and the way he said it, I knew he wanted no part of tending to my mother. Luke was the kind of man who left sick women to female nurses.

"Just drive those cattle down to Lost Creek and tell Ruben Gonzalo what happened here. See if you can't get Julio Selva to round up some men to help us go after those Utes and get my father back."

"That's a pretty tall order, Chip. That's a good twenty mile down to Lost Creek. If the snow flies, you and your ma might be stuck up here. You won't last the winter. We better cart her on down, see if we can't get her a doctor."

"I think the trip would kill her."

"Damn. I don't know if I can drive that herd all by myself."

"Then don't," I said. "None of this would have happened if you hadn't defiled that shrine."

"You blame me for this?"

"Luke, you'd better go now before I start really thinking about that. If you want to help, if you want to try and make up for what you did, you'll get those cattle down to Gonzalo's and bring some help up. If not before winter, then in the spring when the snow's melted. I'm staying up here."

"You trust me?" he asked.

"Right now, Luke, not a hell of a lot."

Luke gave me a dirty look, and then he walked over to his horse. I watched him ride off down into the valley. He'd have sixty head or so to run down the mountain. Some of the time, he'd have the cattle strung out in single file and sometimes, the cattle would scatter. But if anyone could do it, Luke could.

Right then, I just didn't want to see his face.

I was afraid, if he stayed there with me and Ma, I might kill him for what he had done.

21

THAT NIGHT, AFTER I FINISHED UNPACKING EVERYTHING, shucking the panniers from the pack horses and putting all our clothes and such back in place, the sky scudded over with clouds and we got a light dusting of snow. I knew my mother and I would never survive the winter up in the Rockies if I didn't get a lot of urgent things done very quickly. At least my mother's bleeding had stopped, which was a very good sign, I thought, in my ignorance about such things. In fact, when I scrubbed up, after taking her to her bed, I noticed that there wasn't as much blood as I had thought. I think a lot of that had to do with my mother. She had probably lain very still after being wounded and so her blood had thickened and ceased to flow.

That night, I cried for her and hoped she couldn't hear me. I buried my face in my blanket and sobbed until I fell asleep.

The light snow melted soon after the sun came up the next morning. And it turned warm. So I was able to accomplish a lot, although my mother was still feverish and still in shock from loss of blood, perhaps still stunned by her terrible experience. She didn't try to speak, but slept most of the time. She only roused when I spoon-fed her my thick broth.

By mid-afternoon of the following day, I sensed another change in the weather. There was a chill in the air that hadn't been there before, and the wind picked up, began to blow from the north. Not a good sign. I just hoped the chinking in the log house was solid enough to keep the cold wind out until my mother recovered. Perhaps we both might ride down to Gonzalo's before winter set in. I put the horses up in the corral we had built and gave them grain while the chill wind nibbled at my face and snuck in underneath my clothing.

My father had nearly finished the fireplace and had all the stones collected. It was very cold in the cabin that night. I made a rich elk broth for my mother and me and she was able to drink some, but could not chew any of the meat without convulsing in pain. I bathed her and put more salve on her wounds and bound them with gauze to keep the insects from attacking her flesh. She was so weak from loss of blood that I worried she would just waste away unless I could build back her strength somewhat rapidly.

My father and Luke had built a stone cookstove in the kitchen, which was similar to the Mexican horno, shaped like a beehive, with a mud chimney that made it breathe and let the smoke out. In the front room, the stone fireplace lacked only a short stretch of rock through a hole Pa had left in the roof. As long as the creeks ran, I knew I could bring up mud for mortar and such, but if the heavy snows came, and the freezing, I knew that hole would help put us both in our graves.

I finished building the chimney in the main room, chinked it until it was solid and made sure there were no leaks in our roof. Then I began to cut wood and stack it close to the front door. I also laid in logs and kindling inside, next to the fireplace. I checked all the windows for leaks and made sure there were plenty of blankets for my mother and me. I worked until full dark, then stopped to tend to the horses. I heard elk bugling from one side of the valley and, for some reason, the sound gave me comfort.

I didn't know then, but I would not hear the elk bugle any more that year. The next day, dozens of them streamed past our cabin and joined a herd of fifty or sixty that were heading through the valley for the lowlands. It was a majestic sight, but I was sad to see them leave. That night, I really felt all alone, since my mother was still unable to talk much. She was eating more and more, though, and that was encouraging to me.

"Chip. Chip."

I was laying in more firewood when I heard my mother call me. My blood surged with the rapid pumping of my heart. Just to hear her voice. Just to hear her call my name. I had gotten used to the silence in the house so I must have jumped a foot when I heard her voice. Heard her calling to me.

"Ma. I'm right here."

I hurried to my mother's bed and saw her arm outstretched, beckoning to me.

"Chip, my darling," she said. There was still a husk in her voice, but it was much stronger, more clear, less raspy. "Your friend saved my life."

I knelt down next to her, took her hand in mine.

"Huh?"

"Bear," she said. "He was here when they . . ."

I scowled. So Bear had been here, had been part of the attack on my mother.

"I-I'll kill him," I said, without thinking.

"No, listen, Chip. The Utes, those savages. They were going to kill me. Bear stopped them."

"He did? How?"

"He grabbed the wrist of a warrior who was about to

brain me with a hatchet or something. He pushed the man away. They had already . . . they had . . ." She closed her eyes and began to sob. Her body shook as the tears poured from beneath her eyelids. I squeezed her hand, overcome with emotion.

"You don't have to talk about it, Mother."

"No. Bear. I recognized him." Her eyes opened. They were shining with her tears. Her cheeks were wet.

"Ma, I hate to see you cry."

"He spoke to me in English," she said. "Bear did."

"What did he say?"

"He said he'd be back. He said to tell you. He made the others leave. I know he saved me from death. Your friend."

I wondered. It didn't sound right to me. How could Bear, an outcast from his own tribe, stop the Utes from killing my mother after they had already mutilated her? I was suspicious of Bear and my hatred for all Utes, all Indians, was crowding out all other thoughts. I wanted to kill an Indian right then. I wanted to cut Bear's head off for not coming to my mother's aid sooner. I tasted a bitterness that seemed to have boiled up and tainted my mouth. I could taste my own hatred for the Utes.

"He's not my friend," I said.

"Yes, he is, Chip. I saw it in his eyes. I saw the way he made those others leave. His voice was very loud when he spoke to them. And he threatened them with, I guess, a war club. I remember that. I remember all of that so clearly."

I took out a kerchief and wiped my mother's face. Her body went slack and she seemed to sink into the bed, exhausted.

"I wouldn't trust Bear, Ma. I don't."

She closed her eyes for a moment and I sensed that she was summoning up a memory, or trying to draw strength in that brief moment of rest. When she opened them again, she looked straight into my eyes.

"Where is your father?" she asked. "Where's Luke?"

I told her everything that had happened. I didn't tell her that I had killed a man, a Ute. I was still trying to get over that, too. I kept pushing it out of my mind every time it popped up, but I knew I would have to deal with it one of these days. I just couldn't think about it.

"Thank you for taking care of me, Chip," she said. "I'm tired. So very tired."

"Are you hungry?"

She shook her head.

"No. I want to sleep now. When I wake up, I'll eat. I hear you when you come in the cabin, Chip. I hear you chopping wood outside. I'm sorry you have to take care of me like this. I feel so helpless."

I started to say something, but she closed her eyes and her breathing changed. In seconds, she was fast asleep. I let go of her hand and stood up.

I pulled the blanket up close to her neck and rubbed her forehead with my fingers.

I spent the afternoon thinking about Bear, trying to sort out what my mother had told me about that terrible day when the Utes had attacked us. Maybe Bear had saved my mother's life. But what was he doing with those savages who cut her, tried to kill her? How could he drive them away all by himself?

If Bear did come back, there were questions I meant to ask him.

I just hoped I didn't lose my temper at the sight of him and put a bullet in his Ute heart.

22

THE SNOWFALL STARTED EARLY IN THE MORNING, BEFORE dawn. After the feeble sun rose, I kept looking for Luke to come riding up through the valley, bringing me food, medicine, help. I thought he might get Gonzalo or Blaisdell to ride up with him, knowing that my mother and I were trapped up there with winter coming on. I wondered if something had happened to Luke on his ride down with the herd, or whether he had just decided to abandon us.

By late afternoon, I knew Luke would not be coming. Nor anyone else. The snow was falling too fast, too thick. The mountains were as white as ermine, the pine boughs heavy with wet snow. I heard limbs cracking as they broke under the weight of all that snow. It sounded like rifle shots and I jumped every time I heard a branch crack.

I built a fire in the new fireplace and it warmed the entire cabin. There were no leaks and the smoke went up the chimney. From outside, the smoke gave the place a homey feeling. Once it rose above the trees, the smoke turned invisible against the backdrop of the snowy mountains. It wasn't very cold outside but I knew that I'd have to go hunting very soon. I wished I had shot one of those elk that had migrated through the valley. A big elk carcass would have lasted me and my mother a long time. I told Mother of my plan.

"I may have to ride pretty far to find a mule deer or an elk, Mother. I'll wait until you feel better and can get around."

"I got up this morning, Chip. While you were out."

"You did?"

She smiled. "Stop worrying about me. I feel much better."

Mother had changed clothes. She was wearing a loose-fitting shirt belonging to my father. I no longer smelled the scent of the salve I had been using. She got up off the bed and came over to me, held my hand. She squeezed it.

"I'm not using the salve. The, ah, cuts, are scabbing over, Chip. I thought it best to keep myself dry."

"Probably a good idea. What about the pain?"

"It hurts. Especially when I move. But it's starting to itch around the edges, too. That's a good sign."

We walked into the front room and sat down. She sat in one chair and I sat in mine. We both looked at the blazing fire. It smelled good in there and was warm.

"I saw the snow falling a while ago," she said. "It's very pretty."

"Ma, this is not a good situation. We're going to get snowed in and we don't have much food. I took an inventory. We have maybe fifteen pounds of flour, a half a sack of beans, twenty pounds or so, some coffee, onions, sugar, five or six pounds of beets, eighty pounds of potatoes."

"There's some dried fruit, too, Chip. Berries, a few persimmons, apples, apricots."

I laughed.

"Yes, we have a good variety. But not enough to last all winter."

"We'll make do," she said. "We have some dried elk and venison, too."

"I was going to talk to you about that, Mother. I'm going to have to go hunting soon. Maybe this snow will melt and I can ride down a few miles where I might find deer or elk. I'll have to leave you here."

"I know. I don't feel well enough to ride just yet. I'm afraid of breaking open these wounds. I still feel a little weak."

"I might be gone overnight. Two or three days, maybe."

"That's all right. I wish I could help you."

"I dread leaving you alone. The Utes might come back."

"Don't worry. I'll shoot anyone who tries to come through that front door."

She smiled reassuringly.

But we both sat there in silence with our thoughts. Thoughts of disaster. Thoughts of screaming Utes and blood and winter. I looked at the floor where I had found my mother a few days before. All of the blood there wouldn't wash away and the brown stains were a reminder to both of us of what had happened to her. To us.

I could see that Ma was looking at that spot on the floor, too. Her face showed no expression, however. She seemed in a trance.

"I thought I was going to die, Chip. When the Utes burst in here, I was sure of it. And when that one man started cutting me, I thought of you and how sad it was that you were not there so that I could say good-bye. That's what I thought of."

"Ma . . ."

"No, let me finish. I was very calm. Even through the pain, I felt an inner peace, knowing that I was going to die soon. When I saw all the blood, I thought it would be a slow death, and still there was that peacefulness inside me, that great calm as if a ravaging storm had passed over us and left only quiet in its wake.

"Life slowed down for me after that animal was finished cutting me. He held up my breasts and boasted. Oh, I couldn't understand the words he was saying, but I knew what he was saying. The others were grunting and congratulating him. Then, when he took his knife and raised it over his head, I didn't close my eyes. I wanted to experience that last moment of life. I wanted to see him do it. I wanted to see him plunge the knife in my bloody chest and stare him right square in the eyes so that he would know two things."

"What two things?" I rasped, my voice so low I could barely hear it, my heart racing, my blood pumping like water through a millrace.

"I wanted him to know that I wasn't afraid of him, for one thing. And I also wanted him to know that I hated him. I wanted him to feel that hate as he killed me. I wanted him to carry it with him for the rest of his miserable life."

A silence between us, then. I could hear my own breathing. My mother seemed to be looking off into the distance, seeing things that had never been seen before. The room was quiet and it seemed I could hear the tink of snow on the roof. Even the fire seemed to hold its breath and the burning wood stopped crackling.

"I was not afraid to die, Chip. And, you know, I think that Indian knew it. Even before Bear came up and grabbed his arm and dragged him away from me, I think that damned Ute knew that I wasn't afraid of him and I wasn't afraid of death."

"Ma, you're scaring me," I whispered. "You were so close . . ."

She smiled a wan smile. It was a smile of understanding and patience with me, a mere mortal, who had not gone into that deepest darkest cave where death waited like some fire-eyed beast.

"I was worried about your father. If they . . . if they kill him. But now I know he will face death bravely. I'm not worried about Keith."

"How do you know?" I asked, recovering my normal voice.

"Because I think that when you know your death is inevitable, that there's no way to escape it, you find courage way down deep inside you and you can face it without fear."

"I'm not so sure. You're special, Mother. You're a very special person. I-I'm scared of death."

"Why? Because you don't know what lies ahead after that?"

"Maybe because nothing lies ahead."

"Then there's nothing to be afraid of, is there? If there's nothing, then there's nothing. Nothing is nothing. You can't see, hear, feel, remember. It would be as though you were never here, never anywhere."

I shook my head in bewilderment. It was hard to imagine nothingness. But I saw what she was striving to tell me. We were here. And if we were not here, we might be somewhere else, somewhere different, somewhere unknown. But it was a deep subject and I was having trouble grasping it, understanding it.

"I just don't want to think about dying, Ma. I don't want to think about death. Especially yours or Pa's. It scares me."

She laughed, but there was no humor there. It was like a release, as if she wanted to calm my fears because she had none. I don't know where she got her courage, but I was convinced she had plenty of it. And I was also convinced that she was different from the rest of us. She had a strength that I didn't have, that I couldn't even comprehend. She had been through a terrible experience. She had almost died. Yet, she had not been afraid.

"I've thought a lot about fear while I was lying in bed,

trying to recover from all the blood I lost. I was very weak, but my mind was running at high speed. I dreamed terrible dreams, Chip. I thought terrible thoughts. But I thought about fear and what it was. And you know what?"

"What?"

"I think fear is a natural emotion. Something that helps us escape danger. But only if the fear is real and immediate. If you fear something that isn't right in front of you, something that hasn't happened yet, then fear is a crippling thing. It robs you of life before your life is over. So I don't fear the unknown. And now I think I don't even fear the known, the possible. Do you understand what I mean?"

"It's difficult, Ma. When the bear came after me I was scared. I was afraid of death, or . . ."

"Or what? Worse? Being maimed? Eaten? Bitten?"

"Yeah, I think so. I didn't want its teeth biting into my face or my neck. I don't know. It's all mixed up now."

"You got away. You escaped death, Chip. You escaped being bitten and maybe scarred for life. So fear got you through it. It saved your life, perhaps."

"Perhaps."

She got up from her chair and walked over to me. She walked very slowly and stiffly, as if she were in pain or just wanted to keep from opening up the wounds in her chest.

"Chip, don't be afraid. Of anything. Or anyone. When the time comes, and you need courage, you'll find it. Use fear as a weapon, not as a blindfold that robs you of life before you're dead. Use fear to find your courage."

There it was. That word. Courage. I didn't know what it really was, just then. I knew she had it. I knew that I didn't.

All I had, even after listening to her explain her own feelings, was fear.

She walked back to her bed, her steps slow and measured.

I heard the rustle of sheets and blankets and the creak of her bed as she lay back down in it.

I sat there a long time, trying to digest all that she had told me. I sat there, trying to quell the fear in me of what lay ahead. I was going to have to go after those Utes who had kidnapped my father. I had to try and rescue him.

I knew that I would face death. And I knew that I would be afraid.

23

Late in September, Indian summer came to the high country. The sun shone bright and the snows all melted except on the highest peaks and those shadowed places in the forest. Mother was feeling better, gaining strength and energy with every passing day. She came out into the sunshine and looked at all the snowcapped peaks, her face as radiant as the sun.

Water dripped off the eaves of the cabin and from every tree around. It sounded like rain. It was a very pleasant sound.

"It's beautiful up here," she said. "The crisp air sends a jolt of pleasure all through me."

"You know I'm going to have to leave you for a couple of days, Ma."

"You go on ahead when you have to, Chip. I'll be just fine."

We had entertained ourselves in the evenings, when the wind blew cold and the wolves howled outside, by listening to me read Shakespeare's *Henry V.* I probably didn't

read it well, but Mother and I both liked the music of the
language and I liked the boldness of Henry and the way he
pursued Katherine and won her. I had once had romantic
notions of winning Nora's love that way, even though we
both spoke the same language. Later, I planned to read
more Shakespeare, perhaps something in a lighter, though
more bawdy, vein.

I hated to leave Mother alone, but I wanted to lay in
more meat for the winter, and thought, too, I might even
ride down to Gonzalo's and get supplies for us. Mother
said she was afraid to ride that jolting trail and risk breaking the scabs loose on her chest.

"I'll take one pack horse with me, both for the meat I
get, and maybe, if I can make it down and back from
Ruben Gonzalo's, I can bring some staples, fruit, and vegetables back up."

"Why don't you ride down there anyway, and just kill
one of the cattle so you don't have to hunt?"

"I might do that. I really didn't want to ride that far unless
I know for sure the weather's going to hold. I'd be afraid I
might not be able to get back up here until the spring. I
couldn't bear you being up here that long all by yourself."

She didn't say anything and I knew she was mulling it
over. It would be a risk to ride down that far and there
might not even be any cattle there.

"I'm feeling tired, Chip. I'm going back inside."

That's when it happened. As she was walking back to the
cabin, Mother stepped on a slick spot, or perhaps a piece of
ice. I heard her cry out and then heard a thud. When I turned
around, she was lying on the ground, moaning. I ran up to
her. Tears flowed from her eyes and I could see that she was
in considerable pain.

I knelt down to help her up. When I reached under her to
turn her over, my hands felt a hot stickiness. I looked down
and saw that the front of her shirt was drenched in blood.

"Ma . . ."

"Oh, Chip. I've gone and done it now."

I lifted her gently and carried her inside and laid her on her bed.

"The scab must have broken loose," I said. "I'll get some hot water and a cloth."

Her face was blanched, her cheeks completely drained of color. I touched her face and she felt feverish.

The scabs were still there, but there were breaks in them. They were cracked and blood seeped out from those bare spots and underneath some of the other scabbing. I stopped the bleeding, soaked up the blood, and bathed her chest with warm water. Then I applied salve all over and bandaged her.

"Now, you lie still, Ma, and get some rest."

Too weak to speak, she only nodded.

I should have been there, holding onto her arm. Then she wouldn't have fallen. It was my fault. I just hoped she hadn't broken a rib or injured herself internally. It was bad enough that the scab had been cracked in several places. She could ill afford to lose any more blood, either.

I made a thick stew while my mother slept. I was too guilt-ridden to eat. I would wait until she woke up and then try to put something in my hollow stomach.

I saw to the horses and curried Dan. I knew he needed to get out and run, but I didn't want to leave my mother alone. In case she needed me. She hadn't asked for any powders, but she might, if she woke up in pain. I finished with the horses and was walking back to the cabin to check on my mother when I heard a strange sound. I stopped, let my right hand fall to the butt of my six-gun.

A scraping sound. Off in the trees above our cabin where the land sloped up to the plateau where Ute Mountain stood. I ducked behind the woodpile and waited, listening.

They appeared suddenly, emerging from the thick stand

of pines where the flat joined the slope. Bear and Willow, riding ponies, pulling a heavily-laden travois pulled by another pony. There was no sign of Turtle. I stood up.

Bear raised an open hand as he approached, palm out, to show that he had no weapon, a gesture of friendship. He and his wife rode into the clearing. They were both clad in buckskins. They both smiled at me.

"Bear," I said. "Light down."

He spoke to Willow and she led the pony pulling the travois off to the left and dismounted. She tied her pony and the other one to small pines. Bear dismounted and handed her the reins of his pony, which she led away to tie up with the others. There appeared to be a folded teepee on the travois, along with bundles wrapped in deer and elk hides.

Bear and Willow untied two large bundles on top of the others. He picked up one, she carried the other. They walked toward me.

"How is your mother doing, Chip?" Bear asked.

"She is not well. She fell this morning and started bleeding again."

Willow looked concerned. Bear spoke to her. I think it was in the Ute language. I didn't understand a word.

She nodded and then came toward me, holding the bundle up in front of her.

"For you, Chip," she said. "I make."

I took the bundle from her, shook it out. Something fell to the ground and I jumped. I thought it was an animal or two. Bear and Willow laughed at my sudden reaction.

"They do not bite," Bear said. He bent down and picked up the pair of deerskin moccasins. I felt foolish and I know my face turned red. He handed them to me. I shook out the buckskins and held them up, while I tucked the moccasins under my left armpit.

"Willow make for you," Bear said.

"Thank you, Willow. And, thank you, Bear, for saving my mother's life. She told me what you did."

Bear shrugged.

"Where's Turtle?" I asked, a momentary panic upon me.

"Turtle with aunt in Taos," Bear said. "We go there now. Here. You take meat."

I laid the buckskins and moccasins on the woodpile and took the other bundle. I opened the hide and there was a haunch of elk meat.

"You cut. You dry," Bear said. "Good meat. Good food."

"Yes. Thank you for the meat."

"See woman," Willow said. "You take me woman-mother."

I carried the meat, the buckskins, and the moccasins into the cabin, Willow and Bear following me.

"Who's here?" Mother called from her bed.

"It's Bear and Willow, Ma."

We entered the room. Willow went to my mother right away and looked at her for a brief moment. She crinkled up her nose at the smell of the salve on my mother's chest.

She turned to me and Bear.

"You go," she said. "Willow see. Willow make well."

I looked at my mother, who nodded feebly. Her face was still wan and there were dark circles under her eyes. A pang of guilt struck me. Bear and I left the room. I put the meat on a table in the kitchen and carried the buckskins and moccasins out to the front room.

"You wear now," Bear said, pointing to the clothing his wife had made.

"Now?"

"You see fit, eh? Fit good maybe."

Feeling self-conscious, I took off my dirty clothes and put on the trousers. They did fit well. Then I pulled the buckskin shirt over my head. It, too, fit like a glove. I walked around, holding out my arms, looking at the sleeves. There was no beadwork on the skins, but they felt very comfortable. They felt much better on me than my own store-bought clothes.

"Good," Bear said.

We walked outside. He opened the possibles pouch hanging from a shoulder strap and pulled out his pipe and a leather pouch of tobacco.

"Smoke," he said. "Make talk."

"Bear, you speak better English than that. Why are you talking in such short sentences?"

He laughed.

"Bear come from white man world. Speak like Injun."

"You've been down to Taos?"

"Not Taos. Pueblo."

He packed his pipe with tobacco, attached the long, curved stem. He walked out into a place where there was direct sunlight and held up the burning glass, focusing the rays into the bowl of his pipe. Smoke curled up as he drew on the pipe and he motioned me to a log I meant to cut up for kindling. We sat down. He put away the burning glass and handed me the pipe. I tried not to swallow any of the smoke, but it clawed at my lungs anyway. I coughed and the smoke burned my throat and lungs. I handed the pipe back to Bear.

"Ute on warpath," he said. "Much trouble. Ute make war on white eyes."

"What do you mean? In Pueblo?"

Bear shook his head. Then he looked at me with a piercing gaze, his dark eyes glittering like polished agates.

"All gone," he said. "All dead." He sailed his hand in front of him on a flat invisible plane to show me that someone had been wiped out.

"Who's gone?" I asked. "Who's dead?"

I asked, and I dreaded Bear's answer. He wore the face of a mourner at a funeral and his black eyes glittered with some inner fire that might have been stoked in hell.

24

BEAR PICKED UP A STICK AND DREW A LINE IN THE WET earth. Then he drew some squares and rectangles at the bottom, and another squiggly line alongside the straight one. He made a number of holes alongside the squares and rectangles.

"The cattle were there," he said, pointing to the bunch of holes. "From here, the Utes came." He put the stick to the right of the crooked line. "They took the cattle and ran them off. There was a fight from the houses. The man Ruben, he shot the son of Umiya. The son died. Umiya came back and he took the children of Ruben. He skinned them alive. His braves held Ruben and made him watch. They made his wife watch, too."

"That's horrible," I said.

"Umiya said he wanted the man you know, your friend."

"Luke?"

"Yes, that man."

"Where was Luke while all this was going on?"

"This place," Bear said and stabbed the stick into another rectangle some inches away from the line marking Lost Creek.

I pondered where that might be, and then it came to me.

"Blaisdell?"

"Yes, that is the man's name. He has three daughters. Two of them are in season. They are women."

"Luke was there?"

"Yes."

"He was supposed to bring help up here. To me."

"He said to those who live there that you were all dead. You, your mother, and your father."

"That sonofabitch."

"Umiya killed the cattle he did not drive off. He killed them in the creek and he cut up the little girls of Ruben and the boys and the creek ran red with blood. He told Ruben that from that day on, the creek would be a river of blood for all whites and Mexicans who came to that place. He said it would be called Blood River for as long as the sun shines and the grass grows."

I sat there, stunned, shaking my head in disbelief. That poor family, the Gonzalos, and that treacherous bastard, Luke Neeley. I wanted to grab him by the neck and choke him to death. He had abandoned us and he had lied. And he had let our cattle get run off or slaughtered.

"You were there?" I asked Bear.

"No. I came after. The creek was red with blood. It was a river of blood. There were cows all up and down the creek and the little skinned bodies of the Mexican children. And the wife of Ruben crying and tearing out her hair and the man Ruben crying also and beating fists on his chest like a crazy man."

"I don't understand why the Utes did this. Ruben Gonzalo didn't do anything to Chief Umiya. Neither did we."

Bear handed me the pipe again as he blew smoke out from his mouth. I took a short puff and only a little of the fumes got into my lungs. I blew the smoke out right away. Bear drew deep on the pipe and let the smoke out slowly before he spoke again.

"There is someone who watches the place where the sacred things lie," Bear said, speaking very slowly. "That man Luke, he gave the insult to those sacred things. He made water there, the yellow water. So, Umiya, he says this man must die."

"But Gonzalo did not do that," I said. "Why kill his children?"

"Umiya says that all white men are bad. They lie. They steal. They kill the red man. A long time ago, when the Spaniards came to the Ute lands, they brought the magic dogs, and the Ute were very happy and they were grateful. Then other men came, and they had the magic dogs and they killed the Ute and took their women and mated with them and then threw them away. His mother was taken by the white eyes and made to lie on their blankets while many men lay on her and insulted her with their milk and their seed. And then they killed his mother and took her hair and cut off her breasts and made bullet pouches from them. And they cut away her woman parts and laughed at them and wore them on their belts."

We both looked up as Willow came out of the cabin. She spoke to Bear and ran down toward the creek, carrying one of Mother's bowls in her hands.

"Where is she going?" I asked.

"Willow goes to the creek to get the mud and the medicines that grow there. For your mother. She will make your mother well."

Bear's explanation stopped me cold. Did I trust Willow? Did I trust Bear, for that matter? When it came right down to it, I didn't really know these people. Willow was a Ute, and Bear was half-Ute. Yes, he told me he was an outcast, but he still associated with the Ute people evidently. He came and went freely to Ute Mountain and this valley. My mother's life was in Willow's hands. For all I knew, she might be gathering something from the creek that would poison my mother.

"You do not trust," Bear said, as if reading my thoughts.

"Huh?"

"I see you look after Willow. You do not trust."

"Bear, I am not used to your ways. I do not know what Willow plans to do."

"Willow help white woman. Willow help your mother. Good medicine, yes."

The way he looked at me, the way he spoke, made me want to trust him and his wife. I had no reason not to, at that point. Bear had told me things that he could have kept to himself. Horrible things. I had the feeling that Bear was an honest man and that he felt a certain kinship with me, although I didn't know why. Perhaps, being an outcast from his tribe and not warmed up to by the white people, he thought I might be a kindred spirit. But deep down, there was that suspicion in my mind, that tiny flicker of distrust. It lay there like a faint stain on a white tablecloth. At times you could not see it, but if the light was just right, you could.

"So," I said, to get back to what Bear and I were talking about, "Umiya hates the white people. It looks to me like he has no reverence for life. He also killed a lot of cattle. That was senseless and wasteful."

"Yes. He would hurt the white man any way he could, I think. He would kill their cattle and burn their houses and insult their women and children. He has much hate in him, Umiya."

There was hate in me, too, just then. I hated that we had had to leave Texas because of the Comanches. I hated that Nora and so many of our neighbors had been killed. And now I hated the Utes, Umiya in particular. I hated what they had done to those children of Gonzalo and to our cattle. Oh, there was plenty of hate to go around that day and I had my share of it and then some.

"You have much hate in you, too, white man," Bear said.

"Are you reading my mind?"

"Sometimes, it is easy to read the heart of a man. Your heart beats inside your chest, but it shows its blood on your face."

"I hate this killing, Bear."

"You have not killed?"

He had me there. I wondered what he would say when I told him. I wondered even if I should tell him. The moments passed by in silent puffs of smoke from Bear's pipe and in the beating of my heart.

"Have you?" I asked.

Bear nodded and handed me the pipe. I almost didn't take it because I felt just then that each of us was about to take a step that would change everything for both of us. I didn't know if Bear really was a friend, or if he was a spy for Umiya, for the Utes.

I took the pipe and put the stem to my lips. I drew out the smoke and let it smolder in my mouth before I blew it out very slowly. I didn't choke, for once. Maybe I was getting used to smoking. I know I felt calm and the smoke in the air seemed a peaceful sign, like a cloud floating across a blue sky and turning into wispy strands before it disappeared.

"Yes, I have killed men," Bear said. "I have killed two. One was of the Arapaho tribe."

"And the other?"

I handed the pipe back to Bear. He took it, but did not put it his mouth. Instead, he looked down at it, at the tiny tendril of smoke lazing up in a spiral from its clay bowl.

"The other," he said, "was the brother of Sobotar, chief of my tribe, the Capote. He tried to take Willow from me, and I brained him with a war club. Now, I am no longer in the tribe of Capote. But I am made welcome by the Muache Ute, another tribe that is fighting the white men because they do not want to live on the reservation in Denver."

I was beginning to sense the politics of the plains and the mountains, but as it turned out, I only knew a fraction of the problems besetting the Utes and hardly anything about the underlying tensions fomenting even as Bear and I spoke.

"What about Umiya and Sobotar?" I asked. "Are they friends? Allies?"

Bear shook his head. He put the pipe back in his mouth and drew smoke into his mouth and lungs.

"There is talk among the Muaches and the Capotes about joining bands to fight back the white men who are streaming into the San Juan range after the shining metal, what you call gold and silver. But I think they will never come together. And Umiya is an enemy of Sobotar because of me. Because I killed Sobotar's brother."

"So, you are a hated man by almost all of your kinsmen," I said, wishing I had bitten my tongue instead.

"As are you, Chip Morgan."

"Me? Why? They do not know me. I do not know them."

"When you tell me of the man you killed, you will know why," he said.

Then it struck me. And with the knowledge, came the fear. The fear was an icy hand in my innards, grasping, clawing at my stomach walls like some frozen beast suddenly emerged from the depths of my being.

"I killed a Ute brave," I said. "Who was attacking me. But Luke killed two of them before they rode away."

Bear handed me the pipe. The bowl was almost empty, the tobacco nearly burned down to ashes.

I did not draw smoke from it because of the fear that was now at my throat, constricting it like an iron hand closing on my windpipe.

"Umiya knows that you killed one of his braves. And that is why he wishes to kill you, to hang your scalp in his lodge so that the spirits will know that the death of the Capote warrior was avenged. If you are to live, Chip, then you must kill Umiya. That is the only way."

"How can I kill him? He has many men and I am only one. And I'm afraid, Bear. I am not a fighter and I only killed that one Ute because he meant to kill me."

Then he said something in Spanish, and he must have seen the puzzled look on my face because he translated it before I could ask him what he meant.

"If you wish it, this death of Umiya," he said, "you will find a way."

I handed the pipe back to Bear, suddenly sick to my stomach, either from the smoke already swallowed, or the fear that kept growing inside me until it threatened to paralyze me entirely.

"And you will use your fear to make you strong," Bear said. "And you will find a way," he repeated.

How, I wondered, could I face a man who could skin children alive and never bat an eye?

25

MUCH TO MY SURPRISE, BEAR, AFTER CONFERRING WITH HIS wife, Willow, began unloading his travois some distance from our cabin. He laid out the lodge poles for his teepee and I helped him put up his lodge among a stand of tall pines. Later, Willow joined us as we stretched the hides and laced them to the poles.

"Your mother," she said to me. "I will make well. She very weak. Not strong."

"Are you staying up here for the winter?" I asked Bear.

"We will stay," he said.

And so it was. I welcomed the company and Willow's treatment of my mother's wounds seemed to be helping. Willow was right. My mother was very weak. The opened scabs had caused her to bleed again and she could ill afford to lose any more blood. The mud packs and plants that Willow applied to my mother's chest drew out the infection and soothed the angry red swelling that had begun to develop where the scabs had fractured. My mother told me she was very grateful to Willow for her help.

"What she puts on me is ugly," Ma said. "But it's so soothing. I can almost feel my chest healing. And I know I'm healing."

"I don't trust them very much, Ma."

"Why?"

"Because they're Utes."

"They're people, Son."

"If you're happy with Willow being here, I reckon I am."

"She speaks good English. She's good company. She comes from a different world than mine, so I can learn from her."

"She can learn from you, too."

"She does ask me things."

"What things?" My hackles of suspicion were rising.

"Oh, words. What I eat and cook. Things like that. Women things."

"Did she tell you when you could get out of bed?"

"She said I should stay quiet, not move much, for another half a moon. Several suns."

"You're beginning to talk like her."

Mother laughed. "Well, at least we understand each other. She knows what a month is, and what days are. I think she's teaching me a different way of looking at ordinary things."

"What you have to ask yourself, Ma, is what would she and Bear do if the Utes came back here to finish us off."

My mother sighed.

She looked at me with a long reproving look.

"No," she said, "I will not ask myself that."

Bear and I hunted far from the valley, taking pack horses with us. He showed me little valleys where there were still deer and elk and we began to lay in provisions for the long winter. The brief false summer lasted about a week and we brought in plenty of meat. I dug out one of my father's old rifles and gave him ammunition for it. It was a Sharps carbine in .45/70 caliber.

At first, I was just going to loan it to Bear, but he liked it so much and he shot so well with it, I told him he could keep it. Besides, I felt obligated because his wife had made me that pair of buckskins and she said she would make me another, along with another pair of moccasins.

"Good rifle," Bear said. "You good man."

I hoped I wouldn't live to regret my gift to him.

The first of the winter snows came. They came softly and quietly on a windless night when the moon was full. I stood outside the cabin watching the flakes fall, lit by an oil lamp shining through the open door. Orange light splayed the snow around the doorway with a pastel hue. Willow and Bear were inside the cabin talking to Ma in front of the fire.

Bear and I had laid in more logs by the hearth and had stacked five or six cords on either side of the front door. He told me that the Utes would never cut down living trees to use as firewood. They only used dead wood for their fires. I asked him how he felt about cutting down trees that would be chopped and sawed into wood for burning.

"When I walk the white man's path, I am a white man," he said. "I think like a white man, I walk and talk like a white man."

"When you warm yourself by my fire, Bear," I said, "I hope you remember that this white man is your friend."

"I will remember."

We were snowed in for weeks, and some days we never saw the sun. That's when the big gray clouds hovered over the mountains like the bellies of elephants. At times, I felt as if I were trapped, locked in a closet, or imprisoned in a coal bin, unable to climb out. The snow drifted up to the eaves and put such weight against the front door, it took me hours before I was able to open it. I did this by keeping buckets of hot coals near the door at all times, warming it so that I could push against the door until it gradually opened. And then I would shovel for most of a day, clearing a path so that I could breathe and not feel closed in by all that whiteness.

We had plenty of meat, but our staples began to dwindle. Ma wasn't eating much, mostly broth made with elk or venison, sometimes a snowshoe rabbit for variety that Bear had caught in a snare. When she regained her strength I was very pleased and, for once, we had lots of time to talk. I knew she was worried about Pa although she didn't dwell on him. I would just catch her looking sad and wistful every now and then, and at night, I'd hear her sobbing before she went to sleep.

"You must rescue your father, Chip," Ma said one morning while we had breakfast together, a breakfast she had prepared.

"I mean to," I said, with false bravado. "But I don't know how just yet."

"The Utes will come back, Chip. In the spring. We'll both go after them. We'll track them down and get your father back with us."

She was very serious, very determined. I could tell that.

"Yes, I think they'll come back. But there are so many of them."

"Maybe Bear will know where they are. Maybe he'll help us."

"Maybe. I'll ask him."

"I've been thinking about nothing else for the longest time," she said. "There has to be a way to get to this Ute chief, what's his name?"

"Umiya."

"Yes, Umiya. From what Willow tells me, the Utes are very superstitious. Maybe that's how we can defeat Umiya and free Keith."

"I don't understand, Ma. How can his superstitions help us?"

"Talk to Bear. Find out what they are. I have a feeling that Umiya is terribly afraid of something. If we can find out what that is, maybe that's how we can defeat him."

"I don't know that he's afraid of anything, Ma."

"Well, he is. Everyone is afraid of something."

I knew she was right. I was afraid of a lot of things. Right then, I was afraid of Umiya. I didn't see how it was possible to get close enough to him and his tribe to rescue my father. He was surrounded by skilled warriors, men used to killing other men. We were just two people. Even with Bear's help, that made three, four if we counted Willow and I doubted that she would be of any help.

Later that day, I spoke to Bear. I went to his lodge, trudging through some deep snow to get there. The path that we had made was covered up by more snow the night before, and the wind had blown big drifts over every inch of the path to his teepee.

"Bear," I said, "how well do you know your father, Umiya?"

"I know him."

"Do you know if he is afraid of anything?"

"What do you mean?"

"We want to go after him and get my father back with us. Is there a way?"

"Ah, you ask the good question, Chip. Umiya is not afraid of the white man. He is not afraid to fight. He is not afraid to die."

"But he must be afraid of something. Is he?"

Bear placed another piece of kindling wood into the small fire in the center of his lodge. He looked into the leaping flames as if trying to divine some answer to my question. I looked at the flames, too. They were hypnotic, but I could not fathom any oracles from watching them.

Willow sat in one corner, bundled in a buffalo robe. She, too, was staring at the fire.

"There is one thing Umiya fears," Willow said.

Bear lifted his head and looked at her. He did not say anything.

"You know, my husband. You know what Umiya fears."

Bear nodded. But he did not speak right away. He looked back into the fire, then looked up at me.

"I do not know," he said, "if this will help you. But Umiya does have a big fear. He is always guarding against this fear and sometimes he goes into the sweat lodge to find strength against this fear that he has."

"What is it?"

Willow made a sound. It was a low moaning that came from deep in her throat. It sounded like the wind and it sounded like a person who was dying in great pain.

"Umiya is afraid of ghosts," Bear said. "He has seen ghosts. Once, when he was a young boy, he saw the ghost of his grandfather and another time, the ghost of a dead enemy came to him. I think he has seen other ghosts in his life."

Willow stopped moaning. I looked at her and was sure I detected a faint smile on her lips.

Ghosts, I thought. If that was what Umiya feared, then that was the weapon I must use against him.

I didn't know how, but at least I had found a way.

That night, I listened to the wind blowing through the trees. It made a sound like those Willow had made and sent shivers up and down my spine.

The wind gave me an eerie feeling. It sounded like the cries of the dead, like ghosts in the frozen fastness of night. I went to the door and stepped into the night. Outside, there was a stump covered in snow, a stump that was white as a sheet. The shadows made it seem as if it were moving, alive.

Or dead. Like a white ghost, an apparition from the world beyond this one.

If I didn't know better, I would have been sure that I had seen a ghost.

And there was my answer.

26

THE WINTER PLUNGED US ALL INTO A BITTER COLD THAT January. It was an effort to go the outhouse, but I also had to empty the slop jars so that my mother didn't have to endure the freezing winds that blew across our plateau and through the cracks in the slabs Pa had nailed up for siding. The snow froze so that I could walk on it, but that was little comfort. One of my earlobes got frostbitten one morning when the wind must have brought the temperature down to thirty or forty below zero. My ear hurt for days, and every time there was the least chill in the air, it felt as if someone had stabbed a knife into the tip of my ear.

February was even worse, with the snow so blinding we all avoided going outside as much as possible. Bear showed me how to smudge charcoal and ashes under my eyes, which helped some, but the bright snow was still hard on my eyes. Our food supplies dwindled, but Willow brought us some chickpeas, which we added to the stews. She called them "garbanzo beans." They had a meaty taste to them, and were a welcome addition to our diet.

March brought us more snow and more wind. At night we'd hear it howl against the cabin, whistle under the eaves and try like a sniffing wolf to get inside the chinking and freeze us all to death. By then, Willow and Bear were staying with us, their teepee all but abandoned. Ma and Willow talked a lot in the evenings and Ma taught the Ute lady to play whist, a card game I never could cotton to. Bear and I talked about Ute customs and the life he'd had as a boy, hunting buffalo on the plains, stalking the pronghorn antelope and hunting prairie chickens and quail with stones for his weapons.

He seemed to have led a rewarding life in his youth, although the other Ute boys teased and railed at him for his having white blood.

By early April, the sun warmed the earth and we began to see snow melt around the cabin and on the exposed hillsides. The eaves dripped constantly for several days and nights, and the creek roared with water. By the end of the month, more and more of the valley floor became visible and early in May, Ma shrieked when she saw a butterfly flutter past the cabin on golden wings. The water overran the banks of the creek as water from the high country roared and tumbled down the mountain to the plains.

Bear and I rode up to Ute Mountain. I wanted to look at the shrine, despite his warnings that I should not go there. He came along, for my protection he said, and I was glad to have the company. The ground on the plateau was still damp, but Ute Mountain was bare, completely devoid of snow, and so, too, was the opposite ridge and all but the most shady places in the woods.

We approached the shrine, which was in shadow at that time. We had our rifles and I carried my pistol and knife.

The shrine was empty. It had been stripped of all the sacred objects as well as those items we had left there the previous summer. I felt a cold chill as I gazed at the bare rock which had been littered with totems and gifts.

"Everything's gone," I said to Bear.

"Yes. Umiya has been here."

"When? Before winter?"

Bear pointed to the ground. I looked downward and saw the roil of pony tracks and a few moccasin prints near the shrine. They looked no more than a day old.

"Yesterday, they were here," Bear said. "Five ponies. Five braves."

"Why?"

"This place has been fouled by white men. It is no longer sacred to the Capote Ute."

"How do you know this, Bear?"

Bear dismounted and walked over to the bare shelf. There was a crevice where it joined the rock above and he reached his hand inside. That's when I noticed something that looked like a feather just barely sticking out from the rift in the rock. He moved his hand and worked something out from inside the fissure.

Bear turned around and held up two pieces of an arrow, one in each hand. The shaft had markings on it, bands and symbols that held no meaning for me.

"This is Umiya's arrow," he said. "It is broken. This means that this place is no longer sacred. And it means the Ute will make war on those who broke this holy place. It also means something else."

My skin crawled with a clammy chill as if a shadow had passed in front of the sun.

"Something else?"

"Some of the things that were here," Bear said, "belonged once to Umiya's enemies. Bones. Once there was a knife here. A knife with blood on it."

My skin was still crawling with worms and spiders.

"I didn't see a knife here. Much less one with blood on it."

"Umiya cut his dead enemies. Enemies he had killed. He took away their eyes and their hands and their peckers and sometimes their feet. He did not want them to have weapons in the sky world where the spirits go. He did not want them to walk or to talk or to see. So he cut those parts off. He put some of them here so that the spirits could not come back and get them."

"But there were other things here, too. Besides bones and body parts. What did those mean?"

"Those were things with strong medicine. Those things helped protect the parts of enemies he had cut away."

"And the knife? What happened to it?"

"Let us get away from this place. Do you see where the pony tracks go?"

They went through the gap between Ute Mountain and the opposite ridge. They seemed to have come from that direction also.

I nodded.

"They will make a wide circle," Bear said, extending one arm and moving it in a flat-planed arc. "They will join Umiya and go to the valley beyond La Ventana where they will make their summer camp. That is the sacred way, the path they take."

"So, they just didn't ride up here and ride back? They have to come a special way. A sacred way."

"Yes. We go now."

Bear put the broken arrow back in the crevice and I wondered at how precisely he was able to do that, so that it appeared never to have been disturbed. I could see that small piece of feather sticking out in the same way as when I had first seen it.

He climbed back on his pony and we rode back toward

the cabin. He scanned the ground all the way, looking for tracks, I supposed.

"The knife," he said, when we started descending from the shelf of the plateau. "It is a very strange thing."

"Strange?" The hackles on the back of my neck were bristling once again.

"One night, very long ago, Umiya was awakened from his sleep. He said he heard a noise, like the wind, like a ghost calling out for him. He did not know what it was. The fire in the camp was still burning some. He saw, floating over the fire, that same knife and it was dripping with the blood. The knife floated toward him and Umiya got up from his sleeping robes and ran away."

"Maybe he was just dreaming," I said.

"He said he was not dreaming. He said that he was awake."

"And did the knife go away?"

"He hid in the trees and the knife floated into the sky and he did not see it again that night."

"What did Umiya do?"

"In the day, he and some other braves rode to that place at the mountain of the Ute and he took away the knife. He buried it deep in the ground and put big rocks on it and he saw the knife no more."

We rode through the trees, our horse's hooves making no sound in the soft wet earth and just before we reached the cabin, I put out my hand and touched Bear's arm.

"Wait," I said. "There is something I want you to do for me. If you can."

"What is that, my brother?"

I was touched that Bear had called me his brother. Over the winter, I had developed a strong bond with him. He had taught me much and I felt that he was more than just a friend.

"Is there some way you can make Umiya think that his

braves killed my mother? Can you make him believe that you did not save her? That she died?"

"Why?"

"I'll tell you later. I think it's important that he thinks his braves killed my mother."

"I can do this," Bear said.

"You have a friend in Umiya's tribe?"

"Willow has a sister who is married to a warrior of the Capote. She will visit her sister and tell the people that the white woman died in the long winter."

"That is what I want you to do then, Bear. Thank you."

As we rode onto the flatiron of the promontory where our cabin stood and where his teepee peeked out from the trees, I saw something flashing in the sun. I stopped and pointed toward La Ventana.

"What is that?" I asked.

"Ah, they use the talking mirrors. Those are the Capote. They return to the valley beyond La Ventana."

"Can they see us?"

"They know we are here."

"Will they attack us?"

"No. They make their summer camp. They bring the cattle up to the valley. Then they will talk. They will make the war talk, I think."

"Then I have time to think and to plan," I said.

"What do you plan?"

"I don't know, Bear. But I must get my father away from your chief."

"There is one thing you must do, Chip."

"And what is that?"

"Do not let your mother go outside of the house. If Umiya is to believe she is dead, then none of his people must see her in this place."

"I will do that, Bear."

"Good."

I knew Mother wouldn't like being cooped up in the cabin, but I thought I could convince her that, in order for us all to live, and for me to get my father back with us, she would have to be dead.

This is what she said to me when I explained what Willow was going to do:

"You mean that for me to live, I must die?"

"Yes, Mother. From now on, as far as the Utes are concerned, you are a dead woman."

My mother is very wise. She smiled and nodded her head at me.

"For you, Chip," she said. "I will gladly die."

And I knew she meant it. In the literal sense.

27

BEAR AND WILLOW PACKED UP THEIR TEEPEE, LOADED THEIR travois, and left that afternoon. They said they were going to get Turtle and return one day. Bear said that Willow would visit her sister beyond the wall where La Ventana loomed like a large window. We saw no more flashing mirrors that day, and as the sun was setting, I saw elk streaming through the valley below, heading for the high timber. In the evening sky, there were vees of ducks and geese streaming north, a most welcome sight after the long, harsh winter.

Mother stayed in the cabin, but watched Bear and Willow leave through a crack in the door that I had left partially open.

"It's sad to see them go," she said. "Willow was a treasure. My chest has healed completely, thanks to her."

"They'll be back, Ma."

"I fear for them, too. That Umiya sounds like a monster. A tyrant."

"Bear knows how to take care of himself."

"I hope you're right, Chip."

That night Ma asked me to read to her.

"I'm going to read *Macbeth*," I said. "It's my favorite of Shakespeare's tragedies."

"And the shortest," she said. "I loved it the first time you read it to me and your father, back in Texas."

"I think it's a play that we ought to listen to again because I see similarities in Macbeth to Umiya."

"Oh, that sounds delightful, Chip. I can't wait."

Right after supper, I began to read the play. I drank water to keep my throat from getting dry and read the whole play. My mother sat entranced and if I must say so, I never read better than that night. There was so much to it that seemed to echo thoughts in my own mind, thoughts about fear and guilt and the appearance of Banquo's ghost. When I had finished, Ma and I sat there for a long moment just looking at each other, as if letting the entire play sink in and blossom with new insights in our minds.

"Oh, Chip, that was magnificent. What a brilliant man."

"Macbeth?"

"No, silly. Shakespeare."

"What did you think about Banquo? And his ghost?"

"Banquo was an honest man. Smarter than Macbeth. His ghost was powerful. I think it drove Macbeth mad. At least it drove him to kill senselessly. But, I think Banquo's ghost was only in Macbeth's mind. Or maybe it was his conscience. After all, he was the only one who saw the ghost at the banquet."

"Macbeth killed Duncan himself, but he ordered Banquo's death. Nevertheless, he was guilty of murder. He thinks he got away with it and denies that he killed Banquo. That seems much the same situation as with you and Umiya."

"What do you mean?"

"If Umiya thinks his braves killed you, he may feel guiltless in your death. But, if your ghost were to appear at Umiya's banquet, he might take on the guilt and the fear."

"Chip, what are you trying to say?" she asked.

"I'm saying that if Umiya thinks you're dead and he sees your ghost, he may run away in fear. He might make a mistake and we can get to him. Kill him."

"And how do you intend to do such a thing?"

"I'm working on some ideas, Ma. When the time comes, I'll tell you everything."

"Do you think it will work? This idea of yours?"

"I do, Ma. I just wish I had three witches to prophesy for Umiya."

Ma laughed.

"You're asking for quite a lot," she said.

We spoke no more about the play or Banquo's ghost that night, but I could think of little else. I shot a mule deer the next day and we had fresh meat. I knew I'd have to leave Ma alone and go down to Gonzalo's and maybe even to Pueblo to get fruits and vegetables one day. But I was reluctant to leave her alone. She would have to empty the slop jars at night when no one could see her and she'd have to be very careful. La Ventana was just too close and it would be too easy for Umiya to send a war party to our cabin after I had left.

As it turned out, I did not have to leave Ma alone.

I saw them enter the valley below our cabin. It was nearly noon. Three men. The horses gave me the warning with their whickering and neighs. I went inside, grabbed my rifle and told Ma what I had seen.

"Somebody's coming. I don't think they're Utes. You stay inside, Ma."

"Chip, you be careful."

I took up a position behind a tree and waited, holding

my rifle across my chest, ready to cock it and bring it to my shoulder.

The riders were leading three pack horses. Even from way off, I could see that the panniers were heavily laden. I knew then that those men were not Indians. I just hoped they weren't renegade white men invading our valley, hunters come to camp and make meat.

As the men drew closer, I recognized one of the horses. I had seen it at Gonzalo's. My heart soared. Still, I waited, fearing some kind of trick.

Then, as the three riders made their way through the green valley, it became clear who they were. Ruben Gonzalo was there, accompanied by Harry Blaisdell and Julio Selva. They were heavily armed and all had their rifles laid across their pommels. I stepped out from behind the tree and stood on the edge of the precipice. I waved at them, holding my rifle over my head and pumping it up and down.

At first, I thought they hadn't seen me. Then Gonzalo lifted a hand and waved back.

Elated, I ran inside the cabin to tell Ma. She was excited.

"I think they're bringing supplies," I told her. "They're leading three pack horses."

"Oh, I hope so, Chip. Can I come out to see them?"

"No, you'd better stay inside as Bear said you must do. I'll have to make them all swear to keep our secret."

"Who's coming?" she asked. "Luke?"

"No, Ma. It's Ruben, Julio, and Harry Blaisdell."

She looked crestfallen.

"I doubt if we'll ever see Luke again, Ma. And if we do, he's got some explaining to do."

"Don't look for trouble, Chip."

I went back outside and waited for the men to ride up. It seemed to take them hours to ride across the long valley, but soon they were climbing the slope up to the plateau.

I was grinning when they finally pulled up in front of the cabin. All three of them looked at the structure and I could see admiration and surprise on their faces.

"Howdy, Chip," Gonzalo said, in his faintly accented English. "We thought you were dead until that half-breed Bear came and told us you were alive."

"He said you needed supplies," Blaisdell said. "So we brung 'em."

"I am sorry about your mother," Selva said, a sad look on his face. "The half-breed told us about her, too."

"You built a good house here," Gonzalo said. They all looked at the cabin again. They all sat their horses as if to emphasize my impoliteness.

"Light down," I said. "And come on in. Any of that stuff you brought go inside?"

"Near all of it," Blaisdell said. "We got some vegetables and dry fruit and coffee, sugar, flour."

They all dismounted and we started untying the diamond hitches on the panniers. I opened the door, and the men began streaming in. There was no sign of my mother and I figured she was hiding in the bedroom. But I couldn't have that.

"I have another surprise for you," I said. "But first you have to swear that you can keep this a secret."

They all laid their sacks on the table and floor and looked at me, puzzled expressions on their faces.

"Your pa came back?" Gonzalo asked.

I shook my head.

"You have to swear to me that you won't tell anyone what I'm going to show you."

"I swear on my mother's grave," Gonzalo said.

"I swear, too," Selva said, putting a fist over his heart.

"I'll keep your secret, Chip," Blaisdell said solemnly.

"Wait here," I told them.

I went into the bedroom and found Ma sitting on the

edge of her bed. It looked as if she had been holding her breath, which I thought was silly. But she had been trying to stay quiet.

"Come on, Ma. It's Ruben, Julio, and that Harry."

"Do you really think I should?"

"Better they find out this way, than carry their suspicions back down with them. I'm sure they won't tell anyone."

"All right."

She followed me into the kitchen. I watched the men's faces for their reactions.

"Hello," Ma said, her voice sounding very cheery and pleasant, as if she had just walked in from a private stroll. "Thank you for bringing all the food."

A deer haunch hung from a hook in one corner of the room, but they knew what she meant.

Their mouths dropped open. They stared at her as if seeing a ghost.

"But . . . but . . ." Gonzalo spluttered.

"We thought you was dead, ma'am," Blaisdell said, a sheepish look on his face.

"We heard the Utes killed you, Mercy," Selva said, "begging your pardon."

"Thanks to Bear, they did not," Ma said. "Now, don't look so shocked. I may not be as pretty as I once was, but I'm alive and glad to see you men. It's been a long, long winter."

The men laughed, relieving the tension in the room.

"Why can't we tell anyone you're alive?" Gonzalo asked. "My wife will be very happy to hear this after what happened to us."

"I'm very sorry about your children, Ruben," she said. "It must be horrible. Chip has his reasons. He wants Chief Umiya to think his men killed me."

The room got quiet then.

All of the men looked at me as if I were a bug that had crawled out of the woodwork.

That's when I got the idea that all or some of them might be able to help me with the plan that was forming in my mind, getting more precise with every day.

They all continued to stare at me as I summoned up the courage to express my thoughts and ask for their help.

Could I trust them?

I didn't know for sure, of course, but my father's life depended on my plan and my actions. And I needed help. If I couldn't trust these men, I thought, who could I trust?

I studied their faces for several moments, weighing my thoughts, assessing how much I wanted to tell them.

It seemed an eternity before I spoke.

28

I MADE THE MEN WAIT.

We finished unloading and storing the foodstuffs they had brought and then we all ate lunch. Afterward, we sat in the front room. Ma had made tea that Gonzalo had given us and when everyone was relaxed I told them only those things I wanted them to know.

"Umiya makes his summer camp in that valley beyond La Ventana," I said. "I'm going to go up there with as many men as I can get and attack him."

"That's suicide," Blaisdell said.

"He must have more than a dozen braves with him," Gonzalo said. "Maybe more now."

"If enough men could create a diversion, which I have in mind," I said, "I think I can take care of Umiya. If he falls, the rest of his band will run off or give up."

"These are warriors descended from a long line of fighters," Selva said. "And up here in the mountains, the Utes know where to hide. I think it would be very dangerous to go after Umiya with a small force."

"If you don't want to help . . ." I said.

The three men looked at each other as if trying to make up their minds. As if I had accused them of being cowards.

"I will help you," Gonzalo said. He looked gaunt and haggard and I supposed the deaths of his children weighed heavily on him. I could see the sadness in his eyes replaced by a determination. Perhaps for revenge.

"You can count on me and my hands," Blaisdell said. "I'm sure all of them will welcome the chance to clear this country of Utes."

"I know some men who will join us," Selva said, and I knew I could count on him. He was a man of his word and I trusted him. I knew Blaisdell least of all, but I had no reason to doubt him. Still, there was one nagging question I needed answered and had waited a long time for the opportunity to ask it.

"Harry, what about Luke Neeley? Is he working for you?"

Blaisdell's face changed expression immediately. His visage twisted into a scowl as if he had swallowed something sour.

"I ran Luke off my place months ago, Chip. I didn't like him around my daughters, for one thing. For another, I didn't like the way he handled those cattle of yours. He didn't do his job. He left the cattle untended while he chased after my daughters and look what the Utes did, killing Ruben's kids and slaughtering good beef at Blood River."

"Where did Luke go?" I asked.

Both Blaisdell and Gonzalo looked at Selva.

"I saw him in Pueblo," Selva said. "At the time, I didn't know what had happened up at Lost Creek, which is now called Blood River thanks to that bastard Umiya, so I figured you all had come down and found a spread where you could winter your herd. Now that I think of it, the man acted very suspicious, like a man who was hiding something. He told me that you and your mother were dead and probably Keith, too. He said he was clearing out, going back to Texas."

"Is that all?"

"I asked him about the cattle, and he told me he had turned them over to Ruben. The man's mouth was full of lies."

"I always thought Luke was a friend," Ma said. "I never thought he'd do anything like this. Just leave us with nothing. It's almost as if he robbed us."

"Men do odd things when they're afraid," Blaisdell said. "Luke struck me as a man who had looked death in the face and turned yellow."

Gonzalo and Selva both nodded in agreement.

"Do you think Luke went back to Texas?" I asked.

"No," Selva said. "He did not. He fell in with some bad hombres in Pueblo. These are cattle rustlers and thieves from Taos. I think he will soon be a bad man just like them."

Ma let out a sigh and shook her head in disbelief.

"When I think of all we did for that man . . ." she said. "The ingratitude."

"The treachery," I said, my disgust very evident in my tone.

"He will come to no good," Selva said. "Some of those men he rides with now are renegades. They deal with the Capote and the Muache Utes. They feather their own nests and do not care that they are helping the enemy."

"Then it's even worse," Ma said.

"These are very bad men," Selva said.

"Well, I'm not going to worry about Luke now. If he ever comes back this way, I'll deal with him. Now, how fast can you get some fighting men together?" I asked.

"A week, maybe," Selva said.

"My men can be ready in a day," Blaisdell said.

"I will come." Gonzalo patted the butt of the pistol he wore on his belt.

"Good. Now, there must be another way into that valley besides La Ventana," I said. "Gonzalo, do you know of one?"

"I do," Blaisdell said, before Gonzalo could answer. "I've seen the tracks of the Utes all over these mountains and I've followed many of them when they weren't around. Lost Creek branches off higher up. I mean there's a feeder creek that goes into it from that valley. I've been up there, once, and seen La Ventana from the other side. Spooky place."

"Spooky? Why?" I asked.

"Because the valley reeks of Injuns. Utes. You can see where they've set their lodgepoles, where their teepees have sat, killing the grass underneath. It was like riding through a ghost town."

"Can you draw me a map the way you remembered it? Where the lodges were set and all that?"

"Yeah, I could. It's not something I'm likely to forget."

Ma brought some paper and a pencil. Blaisdell took them to a table and began drawing a map of the valley beyond La Ventana. When he finished we all looked at the map.

"It looks pretty clear," I said. "Can everyone here understand Harry's markings?"

Gonzalo and Selva assented.

"Maybe you can make maps for them when you get back down to Lost Creek," I told Blaisdell. "Here's what I want you to do."

I outlined a plan that they all agreed to. It gave me a week to prepare before Gonzalo returned with some items I wanted him to bring back before we attacked Umiya in his stronghold.

"Can you get some signaling mirrors, Ruben?" I asked. "Like the kind the army uses, made out of polished metal, tin or something, with a crosshairs cut in it?"

"Yes. The Utes use those, also."

"I know," I said.

"What else?" Gonzalo asked.

"Bring me a white saddle horse. Also, I need a small can of red paint and a brush."

"Red paint? What do you do with this?"

"Just bring it, Ruben. I'll see you in a week. Then I'll give you three days to come in to the valley beyond La Ventana from Lost Creek. The timing will be very important. Now, how many men do you think all of you can bring?"

After they conferred among themselves, Selva thought they could muster forty or fifty men.

"That should be sufficient if my plan works. And I think it will."

"I hope this isn't a waste of time and won't mean the loss of good men," Blaisdell said.

"You can't doubt me, Harry. Otherwise, I don't want you to come up and bring your hands. This can only fail if we doubt ourselves and our abilities."

"I just want to be damned sure," Blaisdell said.

"Well, be sure now, because nothing's to change up here. I'm relying on all of you to pull this off. I'll do my part. We'll use the signaling mirrors to let me know when I can go through La Ventana and put my plan into action. By the time you get back, Ruben, I'll have everything set, the whole plan."

The men all nodded. They finished their tea. We all shook hands and I watched them ride away, back down to Gonzalo's ranch at Lost Creek. I still couldn't get used to the idea of calling that peaceful creek by its new name, Blood River. I could imagine the horror, but I didn't want to perpetuate it.

When Ma and I were alone, she voiced her concerns to me.

"Chip, you sounded pretty confident. Even I don't know your plan. Are you sure you can overcome Umiya and all those Ute braves?"

"Ma, the way I look at it is this. When we are faced with great challenges, such as this one, we can either walk away from it and live a life full of regret, or we can pick up the gauntlet and face it head on. I know we have to get Pa back and we have to get the Utes out of our hair. If I don't do it, who will?"

She sighed and squeezed my hand.

"I think you'll do it, Chip. Whatever you decide to do. You've got iron in your backbone. I know that. I just wonder what Keith will think when he comes back home."

"He'll be happy, Ma. He loves you. And you love him."

"But I'm not the same woman now. Part of me is missing. He may not like me anymore."

I shook my head.

"You know Willow used tree moss on my wounds and mud and all kinds of things. She healed the knife cuts, but the scars remain. And sometimes it feels as if my breasts are still there. I can even feel the nipples ache as they did when I was nursing you, when you were a baby."

I felt my face flush with hot blood.

"Oh, don't be embarrassed. It's a good feeling. I just hope your father isn't disgusted when he discovers I have no breasts."

"He won't, Ma. Your breasts are not who you are. If I lost a finger, or an arm, I would still be Chip."

She sighed deeply and looked into my eyes. I could see the sadness there, a sadness so deep it gave me a pang.

"A finger or an arm is not the same as a breast to a woman," she said. "My breasts were not me, but they were part of who I am. Part of my being a woman and a mother. Can you understand that?"

I put my arms around her and drew her close. I understood and I knew my father would too.

I just had to get him back, away from Umiya.

And at the moment, I still didn't know how I was going to accomplish that feat.

Deep down inside, I was scared. Really scared. I wondered if I were man enough to do what needed to be done.

At that moment, I truly didn't know.

29

LA VENTANA.

The Window.

So aptly named, the giant opening in the limestone bluffs that lined the ridge overlooking our valley, seemed to me an entry into a forbidden world. The world of the Utes. A place where my father was now, or was soon to be. I got butterflies in my stomach every time I looked at it, and my wonder at what was on the other side increased almost with every passing moment. But I wasn't just gazing at it, I was trying to summon up the courage to go through it and rescue my father.

At night, under the pewter glow of the moon in that high clear air, it seemed like an entrance into the underworld, perhaps into Dante's inferno. I knew that what lay on the other side was the deepest darkest cave where dragons lurked, a place of death, or, perhaps, of life.

"Ma, where's Pa's spyglass, do you know?"

I was searching through the cabin, trying to find it.

I know my father had one and that he hadn't taken it with him when he was gathering the cattle before he was captured.

"I think he kept it under the bed where he kept his spare rifles and old pistols. In a box."

"I looked there."

"He had it wrapped in a cloth. Underneath everything."

I went back into the bedroom, knelt down and pulled the long, deep box back out. I removed everything this time. Of course the spyglass was at the very bottom. It was under a pistol, on old Colt Navy caplock in .36 caliber that I remembered from when I was a boy. The pistol was wrapped in oilcloth and the spyglass was wrapped in a clean flour sack that was, in turn, enclosed in an old yellowed newspaper from Waco that bore the date October 20, 1863. My birthday.

"I found it," I said.

Ma was in the kitchen chopping up vegetables for a stew she planned to make for that evening's supper.

"Good. What are you going to do with it?"

"Take it with me when we go through La Ventana. So I can look for Pa."

I made sure the lenses were clean and took the brass spyglass outside. I pointed it toward La Ventana and saw the window jump into sharp relief. It looked even more mysterious and forbidding when it was magnified.

While we waited for Gonzalo to return, I cleaned my rifle and pistol, made sure I had plenty of ammunition. I curried and combed Dan and made sure all the horses were well grained and watered. I laid out those items I would take into the valley of the Utes.

As it turned out, Bear, Willow, and Turtle came riding up, pulling their travois, before Gonzalo returned. I was surprised and pleased to see them. Ma and I made them feel welcome. I had lots of questions to ask Bear and I wasted no time.

"Have you been to the valley beyond La Ventana?" I asked.

"I have been there. Willow saw her sister and she took Turtle. I did not go to the camp of my people because I am not welcome there."

Ma served tea and some sugar cookies she had made that morning. Turtle grinned from ear to ear when he tasted the sugar. Willow smiled, too.

"Was Umiya there?" I did not eat any of the cookies, but sipped nervously at my cup of strong tea.

"No," Willow said. "He was not there. They say he will be there before the moon is full."

I started figuring in my head when that would be. We did not have an almanac, but I did watch the sky every night and we paid attention to such things because we knew the moon affected those things we planted and the cattle we had raised over the years.

"In seven moons," Bear said before I could count the days on my fingers.

"How many Utes are in the valley now?"

"Five families," Willow said.

"And how many when Umiya arrives?"

"Ten more," Bear said. "And in another seven moons, ten more until there are thirty lodges."

So, I had time, I thought.

"I am going to get my father back," I told Bear.

"I know you are."

"Does Umiya believe that his braves killed my mother?"

Willow nodded.

"All of the people now believe that," she said. "I told them I saw you bury your mother near the sacred mountain. This made Umiya very angry. He wants you to come after your father so that he can kill you both. That is when he will kill your father. When you come for him."

My mother's face blanched and her lower lip quivered. Her hands were trembling when she lifted the cup of tea to her mouth.

I asked Bear if he wanted to come with me when I went after Umiya and he said he would think about it. A look passed between him and Willow, but I could make nothing of it.

He and his family left us. He said he was going to set up his camp near where I had first met him, in the shadow of Ute Mountain. He also said he'd look in on us from time to time and bring us meat.

That afternoon, Gonzalo and two men I did not know rode up. He introduced them as Kerry Reasoner and James Newcomb and explained that they were two of Blaisdell's hands who wanted to look over the country. They were all heavily armed. I told Ruben when Umiya would return to the valley beyond La Ventana and wrote out a message for him to give to Selva and Blaisdell. I told him I wanted all the men to come up the other branch of Lost Creek exactly at 9:00 p.m. on the night of the full moon.

"I hope you know what you are doing, Chip," Gonzalo said.

"I do," I said, hoping that I did not show any signs of doubt.

Gonzalo brought forward the white saddle horse I had asked for, then gave me the signaling mirrors and a small can of red paint and a brush.

"What do you want with the mirrors?" he asked.

"You'll see," I said, not wanting to reveal too much of my final plan.

"And the red paint?"

"I'm going to try and create an illusion, Ruben."

"An illusion? You mean like a magician?"

"Yes. I'm going to become a magician for a little while the night we go after Umiya."

He shook his head, then he and Reasoner and Newcomb left, riding fast through our valley. He knew there was not much time, but before he left he told me that Selva would arrive at Lost Creek in two days with the men he was bringing to fight Umiya and the Utes. I told him I was mighty grateful.

On the night of the full moon, I made final preparations.

Mother objected to what I wanted her to do. Without telling her why, on the previous day I had asked her to sew herself a dress from one of her white sheets.

"Why?"

"You are going to wear it, Ma. Tomorrow night."

"It's a waste of a good sheet."

"Maybe, but it's important. You don't have to make it fashionable, just something that will cover you from your neck to the bottoms of your shoes. It should be loose fitting."

"How loose?"

"Loose enough so that you can run like hell if you have to. And, if there's any wind, I want it to ruffle and wave."

"Chip, I'm wondering right now if you've completely lost your mind."

"I'm wondering the same thing, Ma."

The dress she made out of the sheet was perfect. It flowed when she walked. I had her take it off and then I spread it out on the table we used for dining. She watched me as I brought the can of paint and brush over. I shook the can and then opened it, prying it loose with the tip of my knife. I dipped the brush in it to about a half inch and then started painting circles on the front of the dress.

"Whatever are you doing, Chip?"

"Those are your breasts, Ma. Your bloody breasts."

30

BEAR RETURNED, ALONE, ON THE DAY WHEN THE NIGHT WOULD be bright with the full moon. I was pleasantly surprised and much relieved to see him. I knew that he could be a big help.

"Will you ride with us through La Ventana?" I asked him point-blank.

"In the night, I will go there with you. I will show you the way. I will show you where the camp of Umiya is. Why do you want me with you?"

"I may want you to point out Umiya to me. Is he up there in the valley?"

"You want me to do this so that you can kill him."

It was not a question. I studied Bear's face, but could read no emotion on it. I was asking the man to help me kill his own father. It was a terrible thing to ask of a man and I felt a great weight on my shoulders. I wouldn't blame Bear if he refused to go with us, less if he refused to point out his father, Umiya.

"Bear, it is a question of survival. Ours and my father's.

Umiya wants to make war against the whites. He will not live on the reservation in Denver. He will not leave that valley. If he lives, he will always be a threat to me and others."

"I understand. I have thought of this night long and long, my white friend. I have asked the Great Spirit to light my path, to answer those questions in my heart. I have spoken to Willow. I have fasted and I have smoked. I have sat in my lodge and listened to my heart and in the thunder I have heard the heartbeat of the Great Spirit. I have asked if my spirit will die if I have a hand in the killing of my own father."

There was a deep and resonant silence between us. I felt the sincerity in Bear's words and I was at a loss for any of my own. Yes, I was asking Bear to do a terrible thing, to betray his own father, a father who hated him, probably, but a father who had given him life, nonetheless. I could see that he was waiting for me to say something, to present him with some persuasive argument, to give him some reason why he should go against his own father and, perhaps, be instrumental in his death.

I cleared my throat and prayed that I would find the right words to say to this man who had befriended me, saved my mother's life, and was now tormented by a request I had made without thinking of the consequences.

"Bear, I cannot walk in your moccasins. I cannot enter your heart and I cannot live in your skin or in your brain. I do not know what path the Great Spirit has shown you. I am selfish. I am only thinking of myself and my family. I am much afraid. Umiya could kill me. He could kill my father and my mother. He might even kill you, if you went up against him. I think there will be enough white men helping me so that many of your people will die this night, and perhaps your father as well. All I can say to you is that I will try and take Umiya alive and make him prisoner. But, if I have to kill him, I will not torture him or treat him with cruelty. I am a white man and I live by the white man's laws and I live with my own conscience, which is the voice inside my own heart. If you do not want to help me, I will understand. I would not ask you to take a hand in killing your own father. If he is there, I will find him, with or without you."

"You speak from your heart, as I speak with mine. Yes. He is there. Did you not see the smoke in the sky?"

"I saw the smoke, but I can't read such signals."

Bear grinned.

Ma put on the sheet she had made into a dress, the one with the two bloody breasts painted on it.

"What am I supposed to be?" she asked, when she came walking out into the front room.

"Banquo's ghost," I said.

Bear wore a puzzled look on his face, but I didn't explain. It was already dark and we had a way to ride. I gave him one of the signaling mirrors and told him to wear it around his neck. I had attached leather thongs to the holes in both mirrors and I wore one around my neck.

"Why?"

"I will explain, if it comes to that."

Before we left I had one more thing to do, and I knew my mother wouldn't like it.

"I just want to try this," I told her. "To see how it works. I'll do it again when we get up into that valley beyond La Ventana."

"What?" she asked.

"Close your eyes, Ma. I'll be right back."

I had everything ready. I brought a bowl of water and a cloth and another small bowl filled with flour.

"Now, don't open your eyes. I'm going to dab your face with water."

"Oh, Chip, whatever . . ."

Before she could move, I sprinkled water over her face. Then I flicked the white milled flour on top of it. When I finished, her face was ghost-white. I stood back and grinned.

"Now you can open your eyes," I said, and held up the signaling mirror. "Take a look."

Ma gasped when she saw her ghostly visage in the wavy tin mirror.

"I look a fright," she said.

"Exactly."

31

WE RODE TOWARD LA VENTANA IN THE FULL DARK BEFORE
moonrise.

Bear led the way, with Ma on the white horse right behind him, and me taking up the rear. My mother looked
ghostly even in the blackness of the valley. None of us
talked and Bear rode slowly so that the shod hooves of our
horses did not ring like warning klaxons on stone. It felt
eerie riding toward La Ventana, which stood stark above us
like a window into another world.

We climbed up to the window through shadows and followed a trail along the rimrock to La Ventana. Bear slipped
through on his silent pony and we followed, riding into still
more shadows, with shadows flowing into more shadows as
if we had entered a deep pit.

But we were on high ground and on the far horizon I
saw the tops of the trees softening to silver and I knew the
moon was just below the distant horizon, gliding ever sky-
ward like some ghostly albino eye. Down in the valley,

campfires glowed soft in the blackness, little orange flames quivering like fiery demons risen from the depths of hell, lashing flames like swords or whips, whirling like diminutive dervishes, shooting golden sparks into the air.

Bear reined up and my mother halted the white horse she rode. I eased Dan up next to Bear. He pointed to the fires bristling on the open slope. Some distance from the camp I saw the faint ribbon of the creek gleaming a dull pewter. I nodded and Bear clapped heels into his pony's flanks and glided slowly down the slope onto a dim trail. We followed through thick stands of pine, spruce, juniper, and fir as the moon rose slowly over the rim of the valley.

The skies turned almost as bright as day in the clear thin mountain air and we rode ever closer to Umiya's camp, following an ancient game trail that concealed our movements from those in the bottom of the valley.

Soon, the fires flickered so close it seemed I could reach out and touch them. Bear motioned for Ma and me to fan out as we broke into the open. He stopped just at the fringe of the trees and we gazed down upon Umiya's camp. The bright moon cleared the far ridge and floated free of the earth's high horizon. The creek sparkled silver now, twisting its way down to the lower end of the valley like quicksilver.

I grabbed my mother's bridle and drew her close to me.

"When we ride more into the open," I whispered, "I want you to scream at the top of your lungs."

"I-I can't," she whispered. "I'm scared stiff."

"You must."

I could see her face clearly. I wet it with water from my canteen and sprinkled more flour on it until she looked like a pale wraith suddenly risen from the grave.

"There Umiya," Bear whispered to me. He pointed to a

small chunky man in yellow elkskins laden with bright colored beads on his shoulders, chest, and sleeves.

Umiya was speaking and the other braves were listening. I saw no women or children.

I had a clear shot, but I knew the darkness was deceptive. I needed to be closer. And I needed to test Umiya's mettle when he saw my mother.

"Here we go," I said to Bear. Then, turning to Ma, I said, "We're going to ride straight at the camp at a gallop. As soon as your horse sets out, you start screaming with all your might."

Bear looked at me. I nodded.

"Now," I whispered and buried my heels in Dan's flank. Bear kicked his pony and Ma did the same. Then she screamed as she rode straight for the fires ringing the Utes. Her scream rose to a high shriek and I was proud of her.

Umiya stood up and stared at the apparition riding down on him. The braves sat there, frozen.

Then Umiya screamed. His scream turned into a death chant and he drew a warclub from his beaded belt and held it over his head as if to defend himself.

I rode up alongside Ma and reached out for her bridle. I halted her horse, then brought my rifle up, cocking it on the rise. Umiya looked at my mother and his chanting screams died in his throat. Ma waved her arms and the sheet she wore rippled, bright white in the moonlight.

Umiya turned tail and ran. I shot him in the back. Then I saw where he was headed and my heart leaped up into my throat. There was my father, tied to a tree, his face covered with beard, his eyes wide with fright.

The Ute braves started running toward their horses at the lower end of their camp, but rifle fire crackled like Chinese firecrackers and the braves started falling grotesquely.

Riders appeared out of the darkness, their horses and

bodies limned by the moonlight, their rifles flashing orange fire as they swarmed over the frightened Utes.

I raced down to my father and Umiya rose up before me, blood gushing from the exit wound in his chest. I levered another cartridge into the chamber and shot him down, the rage in me overcoming my fear.

"Chip," my father gasped, struggling to free himself from his bonds.

I hit the ground running and then my knife was slashing at my father's ropes. He pulled free of the tree and his wobbly legs gave out. I grabbed him before he hit the ground and held him close to me.

I heard a low keening sound. When I turned around, there was Bear squatting on the ground next to Umiya, singing his father's death song. Tears streamed down Bear's face, tears that tugged at my heart.

The firing died away and my mother rode up, looking down at us.

My father's mouth gaped open in horror at the sight of her.

"Mercy?" he spluttered.

"Yeah, Pa," I said. "It's Ma."

"I thought you were dead," he said. "Is that really you?"

She laughed then and climbed from the white horse. She grabbed Pa away from me and embraced him, holding him tight to her, kissing his face and neck, sobbing with happiness.

"The Utes cut off my breasts," she said, her words laced with sobs, tears streaming through the flour on her face, turning it to paste.

"I don't care," he said. "You're alive."

"And so are you, Keith. Thanks to Chip."

The look on my father's face was worth all the gold in the world, all the cattle in Texas.

"I'm right proud of you, Son," Pa said.

I melted inside and I knew my fear had melted as well.
When I saw Umiya flee in fear, knowing that he was afraid
of an illusion, I felt a sudden rush of knowledge, a revela-
tion that came upon me like a bright light.

Fear, I knew, was something a man made inside himself.
And, so, too, was courage.

Spur Award-Winning Author

Jory
Sherman

Texas Dust

When Joby Redmond returned from war,
he thought he had put the killing
behind him. But when his lifelong
enemy appears—and begins terrorizing
the Redmond family—Joby knows
the fight is far from over.

0-425-19430-2

Available wherever books are sold or at
www.penguin.com